jUST YOUR AVERAGE PRINCESS

JUST YOUR AVERAGE PRINCESS

Kristina Springer

FARRAR STRAUS GIROUX

New York

Copyright © 2011 by Kristina Springer
Distributed in Canada by D&M Publishers, Inc.
Printed in the United States of America
Designed by Roberta Pressel
First edition, 2011
1 3 5 7 9 10 8 6 4 2

macteenbooks.com

Library of Congress Cataloging-in-Publication Data
Springer, Kristina.
    Just your average princess / Kristina Springer.
        p.   cm.
    Summary: Working in her family's pumpkin patch every year, seventeen-year-old Jamie
has dreamed of two things—dating co-worker Danny and being crowned Pumpkin
Princess—but her beautiful and famous cousin Milan's visit may squash all of her hopes.
    ISBN: 978-0-374-36150-1
    [1. Interpersonal relations—Fiction.   2. Pumpkins—Fiction.   3. Cousins—Fiction.
4. Farm life—Illinois—Fiction.   5. Illinois—Fiction.]   I. Title.

PZ7.S7684575Jus 2011
[Fic]—dc22

                                                                    2010036250

To my four little pumpkins:
Teegan, Maya, London, and Gavin

jUST YOUR AVERAGE PRINCESS

1

Thump.

    Thump.

    Thump, thump, thump.

    "What the——?" The redheaded woman standing across from me at the checkout pales and her dark brown eyes widen. She's looking at something over my right shoulder.

    It takes me only a fraction of a second to turn, but it feels like everything is moving in slow motion as I take in the full scene.

    "Avalanche!" I scream, racing for the huge pumpkin-tower display near the entrance to the Patch. Pumpkins are rolling down the sides of the tower from the top and people are yelping and jumping out of the way as the twenty- and thirty-pounders barrel toward them.

    A woman screams, both her arms extended over her head

like she's on a roller coaster. I look up into the sunlight at the peak of the tower and my eyes focus on the cause of both the scream and the avalanche.

A little boy.

His arms are out to his sides in a shaky *T* as he balances on the top pumpkin.

I don't think. I don't speak. I don't hesitate.

I run. I sprint up one side of the pumpkin tower, taking two pumpkins at a time until I'm at the top. Without pause, I grasp the little blond mountain climber under my right arm and jump off the back of the tower.

There are several yells of "No" and "Oh my God" and I can hear a number of women gasp, but I know what I'm doing. This isn't the first time a kid has climbed the pumpkin tower.

I bicycle-kick in the air like a high jumper on an all-star track team and land safely on a big fluffy pile of hay, Junior still safe in my arms.

Strategically placing the hay pile here was my idea two years ago when Jimmy Norton climbed the pumpkin tower, causing the first avalanche and my landing to be not quite so pleasant. I keep telling Dad that while the pumpkin tower looks cool, it's way too dangerous. And the hand-painted PLEASE DON'T CLIMB THE PUMPKINS sign posted in front of it is pretty ineffective since most toddlers can't read. But year after year he erects it anyway because he says half the crowd comes just to see the tower. Which I suppose is true. It is one of the popular picture-taking spots here.

Junior's mother is standing in front of me now, trying to catch her breath. Her cheeks are red and tear streaked. "My baby, my baby," she sobs, scooping the boy out of my arms and into her own. She nuzzles her face into his neck and then looks back down at me. "You saved him," she says, her eyes filled with relief and gratitude.

I smile and my heart swells.

"How can I ever thank you?" the woman asks. "Can I give you some money?" She jams a hand into a large striped diaper bag slung over her shoulder while the other still cradles her boy.

I wave one hand in the air. "Oh no, no. Really. It was no big deal. Go on and have a great day with your son."

"Thank you," she whispers, and walks away. Her son grins mischievously at me from over her shoulder and I shake my head at him.

I close my eyes for a second and lie back in the hay. I wiggle my body parts one by one to see if anything hurts. Nope. All good. I landed well this time.

"Jamie? You okay?" a deep voice asks.

My eyelids flutter open and the sunlight momentarily blinds me. But then I make out the unmistakable hazy figure hovering above me.

And my heart beats faster. Danny.

He kneels in front of me and takes both of my hands in his, gently pulling me into an upright position. He smells like a mixture of grass, Doritos, and Altoids. In other words, heaven. I consider falling back into the hay so that we can have us a little redo. But that might be a tad dramatic.

"I . . . I think so," I say carefully. I'm totally fine but I don't want him to go away yet. Or ever.

His hand comes toward my face and for the briefest second I think he's going to grab me and kiss me passionately, overcome with the momentary fear of almost losing me forever. Yeah, I DVR a lot of daytime drama and that would definitely happen next if we were on a soap opera. But he carefully pulls hay from one of my pigtails instead. And I have to say, this is the second-best thing he could do right now, right after kissing me.

"That was awesome," Danny says, standing up.

A small wave of disappointment comes over me. I was hoping we could stay down here for a while.

"Man, it looked like your feet barely touched the pumpkins," he adds.

Well, that *is* the secret during a pumpkin avalanche. If you are quick enough, you can climb to the top of the tower before the pumpkins barrel to the ground. It's kind of like running up an escalator backward. Only faster.

But I only reply, "Yeah."

"How about I help you put the tower back together?" he asks, eyeing the pumpkins scattered all over the place. Patrons entering the Patch are stepping around the mess and throwing one another puzzled looks. I glance over at the three registers under the green-and-yellow-striped tent where I'd been working. Phyllis, one of our part-timers who has been working here since I was in diapers, took over my register for me and is handling the long line of customers waiting to check out with their pumpkins.

"That'd be great," I reply in a voice a little more breathy than I'd like. But hey, I just jumped off the back of a pumpkin tower, I'm allowed to be a bit winded.

Okay, normally I'm what you'd call a "talker," as in, I like to talk. Constantly. To everybody. Customers, people at the post office, grocery store clerks, other students at school. In fact, the only trouble I've ever gotten into at school has been for talking. I'm a repeat offender. I can't help it! I like to socialize. You'd think that was a healthy thing, right? But when it comes to talking to Danny it's like my heart is sucking all the blood from my brain and I can't put more than a few words together.

Yeah. He's that cute.

I've always thought I was pretty tall at five feet eight, but Danny is a good six or seven inches taller than me and built like a baseball player, muscular and slim. And he's got this smile that melts my insides every single time I see it. I've been in love with him since I was thirteen and first started working at the Patch. That's four years of solid devotion.

I remember the day, really the very second, that Danny

stopped being just another Patch worker and started being the guy who could make my heart thump out crazy beats. It was late August and a half dozen or so seasonal workers and I were out in the field, loading the wagon attached to Danny's tractor with pumpkins to bring up front for the displays. He was sixteen and a part-timer at that time. I was pretty tiny back then and the other workers were loading much faster than me. One of the older girls called me Squirt and said I should stick to loading the small pumpkins. Well, I didn't like being called Squirt so I went after the biggest pumpkin I saw. It had to be a good forty to forty-five pounds. I picked it up and started making my way slowly to the wagon. The pumpkin was heavy and the next thing I knew I lost my balance and fell over backward. The pumpkin tumbled over my shoulder into the dirt and I got a nasty scratch on my cheek from the stem. I bit down on the insides of my cheeks, determined not to cry and look like a big baby in front of everyone. Danny came over, looked at my face, and brought me to the driver's seat of his big green tractor and had me take a seat. He pulled out a first-aid kit and set to cleaning and bandaging my scratch. I didn't say a word while he worked and I didn't even cringe when he put on the stinging antiseptic. I watched him concentrating on my cheek and how the corners of his lips curled up slightly like they might turn into a smile at any given moment. Suddenly my skin got prickly, I felt flushed, and my heart was pounding in my ears. That's when I knew I was D-O-N-E, done. Danny was then, and still is, the only target of my affection.

Danny hoists a fat orange pumpkin under each of his arms and heads for the center of the collapsed tower. His gray flannel sleeves are rolled up and his tanned biceps are flexed.

I *so* wish I had my digital camera right now. I would capture this moment, blow the picture up to a monster-sized poster, and hang it over my bed. Or maybe I'd take a bunch of shots and make a calendar. Twelve months of Danny. Wow. This would be the shot for October, my favorite month.

Time to stop daydreaming and get to work. I wipe my sweaty hands on my overalls, scoop a pumpkin into my arms, and follow him to the pile.

The avalanche-watching crowd has dissipated now since there isn't anything to see, just a mess to clean up. The parents pull their small kids in old red metal wagons and head for the petting zoo or the pony rides or the caramel apple stand. During pumpkin season, people come from all over to visit the Patch, even as far out as Chicago. It's tradition to a lot of folks. Not to mention all the school field trips, Scout troops, church groups, and people who want to hold picnics and parties here. There are a hundred things to do at the Edwards Pumpkin Patch; it's 160 acres of fun and I've loved it my whole life.

I look over at my best friend, Sara, who is working at the caramel apples, and feel myself blush. Sara is making this incredibly obnoxious kissing face and passionately hugging herself. Sheesh, I hope no one else sees her. She can be such a freak. I turn back to see if Danny noticed, but he's busy scooping up two more pumpkins.

"Stop it!" I mouth at her, and she laughs. Sara knows all about my long-term crush on Danny. She's always telling me to ask him out already. But I can't do that. Geez, what if he said no? I'd be so humiliated and never be able to face him at work again. Which means I'd have to quit, thus losing all my spending money, not to mention the ability to pay for gas for my car. And, furthermore, ruining my social life since cruising is the number-one Friday night teenage activity in the town of Average, Illinois. True, my family owns the Patch, but Danny is a full-timer now and they need him here to do a lot of the heavy work with my dad. Sure, I'm family, but if it came down to who would keep their job at the Patch, I'm pretty sure Danny would win. People come to the Patch and see what a huge operation it is but I'm not sure they know that most of these workers are seasonal. During pumpkin season, Dad hires anywhere from seventy-five to a hundred seasonal workers. But as for the rest of the year? He only has ten part-timers and a handful of full-timers. He needs Danny.

And, ugh, what if Danny has a girlfriend? Though I'm almost certain he doesn't. He works too hard to have time for a girlfriend. One outside of the Patch anyway. He's always here, taking whatever overtime he can get. He's saving to buy his own land. He wants to run his own farm one day. Man, having goals is so sexy.

Danny looks over at me and smiles. I almost drop the pumpkin I'm holding, but I manage to smile back, wishing my smile could convey what's in my heart, like: "You're wonderful." "You're gorgeous." "Please, please, please ask me to go on a date!" But there's no heart-to-English translator around and Danny picks up two more pumpkins and heads for the tower.

We stack in silence for a good twenty minutes. I'm moving slowly enough to prolong the job as much as possible, but not so slowly that Danny thinks I'm a poor worker or a weakling. Whenever I can, I sneak glances at him, admiring tiny things like how he lets out a small grunt every time he hoists up a couple of pumpkins. And how he rubs his cheek on his shoulder instead of reaching up and scratching it with his hand. And how his messy brown curls hang almost completely in his hazel eyes. Every few minutes he gives his head a little shake to knock them out of his way. It's completely adorable.

I want to make a connection with him, something that will make him take notice of me as more than just Henry Edwards's daughter, but I don't know how. I keep trying to come up with something witty or interesting to say.

Something.

I'm about to ask him if he's seen the YouTube video of the cat that can sing "La Bamba" when Danny says in a low voice, "*Who* is that?"

I turn in the direction of his gaze and see a long tanned leg in a fancy-looking shoe come down from behind the passenger door of my dad's beat-up old truck and land smack-dab in a giant mound of pumpkin guts.

There is a shrill shriek followed by "Ew, ew, ew!"

The other leg of the shrieker joins its match. She's here.

"That's my cousin Milan," I say to Danny, not taking my eyes off her.

2

It's so good to see you!" I exclaim when I reach Milan. And it really is. We haven't seen each other since we were kids and argued over whose Barbie got to marry Ken. She won because I didn't like to fight. Her Barbie was more the domestic type anyway. Mine wanted to be an astronaut. Though Ken did flirt with my Barbie whenever hers was busy with a clothing change. I hold out my arms to Milan for a hug.

"You've got to be freaking kidding me!" she screeches. "Who leaves a pile of disgusting orange mush lying out on the ground like this?" Milan bends down and slips a three-inch heel off her right foot and examines it.

It's a pumpkin patch, I want to tell her. There are pumpkins everywhere. And sometimes there are rotten ones. It happens. But I'm getting the feeling she wouldn't react well to me pointing this out to her just now.

I am beginning to feel silly still holding my arms out and she is apparently not in the hugging mood so I put them back down at my sides.

"Oh my God, would you look at this?" She shoves a coffee-colored shoe with the cutest pink polka dots on it at me.

The shoe is badly stained from the pumpkin guts. I run my finger over one of the pink dots to see if any of the guts comes off. The leather feels so smooth, like freshly lotioned skin.

"Well, maybe we can wash it," I say, and she looks at me like I'd told her she would be sleeping in the barn with the goats.

"You can't *wash* Roy Vances! They're ruined!"

She looks completely distraught and I want to say something to make her feel better. My dad climbs down from the driver's seat, shaking his head. He slams the driver's-side door shut and heads toward the house, leaving Milan with me.

This is definitely not how I wanted Milan's visit to start. She seems superupset. "We have a Megastore about a mile from here. Maybe we can find something similar?" I suggest.

Milan stops ranting and cocks her head at me. And then she starts laughing. Really loud.

I smile, waiting for her to stop laughing and fill me in on the joke. "What?" I finally ask.

She wipes at the tears in the corners of her eyes. "Roy Vances *start* at around two grand. I don't think your 'Megastore' will have them."

Two *thousand* dollars? She's got to be kidding. My car didn't even cost two thousand dollars.

"Thanks for the laugh though. Jamie, right?" she asks, eyeing me up and down.

I nod, surprised at the question. I know it's been a long time since we've seen each other, but hasn't she seen any recent pictures of me? I've seen loads of pictures of her so I knew exactly what she looked like. Of course, those *were* mostly tabloid shots. But still. Surely she's seen our family Christmas letters over the years. Mom works so hard on them.

Milan bends over and plucks off her other shoe. "Here, Jamie. Toss these out for me, okay?" She drops the shoes in my hands and turns toward the house. "So I take it this is where I'm staying?" she calls over her shoulder as she follows the path my dad took.

Wow. That went quite a bit differently from what I expected. I'm still standing at the open door of the truck, holding Milan's shoes, and I can feel people watching the scene. I glance at the caramel apple stand and see Sara gaping. I look at Danny standing in front of our newly erected pumpkin tower with his arms crossed and a big smile on his face, watching Milan walk away.

I feel a little sick.

~

I start to toss Milan's shoes into one of the huge green garbage cans spread throughout the Patch, but then reconsider.

They're too expensive to throw away. And what if she changes her mind? No, I'll keep them somewhere for her. I follow Milan, about fifty yards behind her, to the house, stopping briefly to hide the shoes in a bush until I can bring them into the house later.

There's something bothering me and it's not only Milan's odd interaction with me. Why did Danny look at her like that? I wonder if he recognized her from her pictures. Milan's not in the tabloids every week or anything, but occasionally the paparazzi will get a shot of her. Aside from being gorgeous, she's the only daughter of two A-list movie stars in Hollywood—Jack and Annabelle Woods. Uncle Jack and Aunt Annabelle to me when I see them. Which is just about never. Uncle Jack is Mom's older brother by three years. They grew up here in Average, Illinois, but he ran off to Hollywood to act, the first chance he got. And Mom met Dad senior year in high school and married him a couple of years later. Mom has almost never talked about Uncle Jack, not until recently anyway. I think she's always been either mad that he moved away and left her at home alone with their parents or jealous that he's so famous. I'm not sure which. It could be both, for all I know. But then recently she's been whispering to Dad a lot and I've heard her say things like "Jack thinks . . ." and "Jack's worried . . ." and "God forbid she turn out like her mother." Okay, that last one could have been about anybody and not about Milan. But all I know is, suddenly my cousin Milan, whom I haven't seen since we visited her family when I was six years old, is staying with us and helping out for the entire pumpkin season.

I kick my boots at the block of concrete with the metal scraper sticking out of it, knocking loose dirt from the Patch, and then push open the old wooden front door with the ripped screen and walk into the house. Mom's got both of Milan's tiny hands in hers and she's gushing all over her.

"Oh, sweetie, oh look how much you've grown up! You're a young woman now!" Mom says, a huge smile spread across her face. I notice Mom has set her hair and put on a little makeup. She's wearing a pale yellow shirt with a long skirt. Not the usual dinner attire around here.

Milan nods. "It's nice to see you again, Aunt Julie."

Mom hugs Milan tightly and Milan twists up her face like she's getting squished. "Oh, honey," Mom says. "Oh, you're much, much too skinny. Don't your parents feed you? Well, we'll fix that right up. I'm making a big dinner tonight. Chicken, potatoes, green beans, biscuits"—Mom ticks food off on her fingers—"creamed corn, and peach cobbler."

Yum. Mom is an awesome cook. I head for the sink to wash up.

Milan looks alarmed. "Um, I'm sorry, Aunt Julie, but I don't eat meat. Or carbs. Or sugar. And I'm not sure what creamed corn is, but I make it a general rule not to eat anything with the word 'cream' in it. And you know corn is a filler anyway, right? Do you have any tofu? Maybe a soy burger?"

Mom looks at Milan for a long minute and her smile disappears. But she doesn't say a word. Finally she turns around, walks to the pantry, pulls out two cans of creamed corn, and walks to the can opener.

Creamed corn it is, then.

My mom's chicken is so good. I mean, so, so good. She always debones it and cuts off the fat, because she knows that rubbery stuff grosses me out, and then she batters it in flour and egg and bread crumbs and fries it in some vegetable oil. Delish. I want to reach for a third piece. I worked hard today and I'm pretty hungry. But I don't want to look like a total pig in front of Milan. All she has on her plate is a scoop of green beans, which she is ever so slowly nibbling on. And that is only after she brought them to the sink and washed each bean individually to get off the butter Mom had added to them. Oh man, I thought Mom's head was going to explode when she did that.

"What are your plans for tonight, Jamie?" Mom asks. She picks up her and my dad's empty plates and turns for the kitchen.

"The usual," I say to her. "Hanging out with Sara."

Dad grunts and pushes back from the table. We watch him leave without saying a word. I'm sure he's off to hole up in his office and watch TV. He's not what you'd call the world's best conversationalist. I'm pretty good at translating his grunts though. That one means "I wish you'd hang out with someone other than Sara every once in a while." Not that he dislikes Sara or anything. I mean, he hired her to work at the Patch and gives her free rein to do her creative thing with the caramel apples. It's only that she's nineteen and out of high school and he'd probably be happier if my best friend was seventeen like me.

And, well, he sorta thinks she's a bad influence on me. Which she's totally not. But it's a small town and everyone knows everything about everyone else so when a rumor gets going it spreads through town fast. I know Dad wasn't too happy when he heard that Sara got caught in a compromising position with a boy under the bleachers at the football field her senior year. But that was two whole years ago and it's not like I followed suit or anything. I don't even go to football games. I work on Saturdays.

And truth be told, there was that one time when Sara first got her driver's permit and we went joyriding in her dad's new truck when we were supposed to be having a sleepover at her house. Nobody would ever have known if we hadn't run out of gas about two miles out of town. We had to call her dad to come get us in her mom's minivan, which he had previously sworn never to step foot in for as long as he lived. Guys are so weird about minivans around here.

But aside from that extremely short list of typical teenage deviance, Sara and I are good people. It's not like we're getting drunk at parties or starting fires in empty parking lots. There are worse people I could associate with. Of course, I could bring Dilly Hanson around more. She's my school best friend. But then Dad would find something wrong with her too, I'm sure. Dilly's parents are a tad bizarre. Not bizarre in a bad way, I mean, they're supernice people, have good jobs, and contribute to the community, and Mrs. Hanson is on the town board. But they do some odd things too, like their house is pink with orange shutters, they hang candy from the tree in the front yard every Halloween, and they named their three kids Dilly, Fraction, and Nero. In a town of only a thousand people, this kind of thing sticks out. I think of them as colorful while Dad says they're freaks. That's mostly why Dilly is my school friend; I don't bring her home too often. I think Dad just doesn't like me having fun.

"Why don't you take Milan with you guys, honey? Show her around Average." Mom walks back into the room, slipping on her sea-foam-green apron with tiny blue flowers around the edges in preparation to do the dishes.

I look at Milan. "Sure, that'd be great." Spending some time together outside the house and away from my parents will loosen Milan up a bit and give us a chance to talk about old times.

Milan looks like she ate a bad bean.

"Um, that's okay, Aunt Julie. I should probably unpack. Or something," she says.

"Plenty of time for unpacking tomorrow," Mom replies, carrying the last of the chicken from the table.

"Yeah, you should come. It'll be fun," I say once we're alone. I start thinking about the places in town I want to show Milan.

Milan pointedly looks from one of my pigtails to the other and I self-consciously reach up and touch one. What, is she worried about my hair? Is there still hay in it? I forgot to check it when I came in. Or is it my pigtails? It's not like I won't do my hair before we go out. All of the girls at the Patch put their hair up. Well, those doing physical labor do, that is. It's sweaty work out there. You don't want your hair sticking all over your face.

Milan chews on another green bean and swallows. "What do you do on a Friday night around here anyway?" she asks, looking the teensiest bit intrigued.

"Usually we cruise the strip. You know, the main drag through town. Everyone does it. You get to see lots of people."

"So, you just drive? Do you ever stop anywhere or is that all there is to it?" she asks.

"Well, no. We mostly drive around. But sometimes when we're really bored we'll drive out to the cornfields and turn our headlights off. It's *so* crazy." I shake my head and chuckle. "There are no lights out there so you are literally driving in pitch-black."

"Crazy," Milan says flatly.

"Um, and sometimes, we'll stop and gather a bunch of ears of corn and then drive back to the main drag and chuck the corn at people out on the sidewalks." Milan gives me an alarmed look. "Not to hurt them of course," I quickly add. "I mean, we don't actually hit people, we just throw it sorta near them. You know, to scare them. To be funny . . ." I trail off.

"You're telling me," Milan says slowly, "that you people throw *produce* at each other? For fun?" She pushes back from the table and heads for the guest room. "What freaking planet have I landed on?" I hear her mumble under her breath before she shuts the bedroom door behind her.

I stamp the last of my potatoes on my plate with my fork. Sheesh. What's with the "you people" stuff? It's not like we're throwing cucumbers and cabbage at each other. It's only the corn. There's loads of it around here. And it isn't like we do it all the time. Just when we're *really* bored. We don't hurt anybody. It's silly. And it's usually Sara's idea anyway. She's the one who throws the corn. I'm always driving. Geez, this *is* sounding more and more stupid, even to me.

An hour later I pull up, alone, in front of Sara's white two-bedroom house with the peacock-blue shutters and dove-gray door, and tap on the horn three times, my signal to let her know I'm here. Sara's mom peeks out from behind the living room curtain, her hair in pink foam rollers, and waves to me. I return the gesture. Mrs. Erickson is so dependable. Every night by 6:30 she's got a head full of rollers and is sitting at the small table in the window reading *Soap Opera Digest*. While I do love my soaps, I don't touch that magazine. I hate how they tell you what's going to happen weeks out. Like, which one of these three *Destined Days* stars will survive a tornado that devastates the entire town only to find out she's got terminal cancer?

22

Spoilers much? I can't see Mr. Erickson from the driveway but I'm 99.9 percent positive he's watching reruns of old game shows from his recliner. It's hard to believe they rerun that stuff but they do. I know Sara is dying to move out, but she doesn't know where she wants to go or what she wants to do yet. She tried community college for one semester last year and absolutely hated it. She said she was never going back. She's not the books-and-studying type.

A few minutes later Sara comes bounding down her front steps, pausing briefly in front of the maroon and yellow mums that line both sides of her walkway. Yellow and maroon are the Average High School colors so I like to tease Sara that her landscaping is the equivalent to having dozens of cheerleaders with their pom-poms sending her off and welcoming her home each day. She pulls a couple of buds from one of the maroon mums and slides into my passenger seat. She pushes one flower behind her ear and hands me the other. But I'm not really in a flower-behind-the-ear mood just now.

"So, what's the plan?" Sara says, buckling her seat belt.

"I don't know," I reply, staring straight ahead at my steering wheel.

"Main drag?"

"Nah."

"Chuck corn?"

"No!" I say more adamantly, as I put the car in reverse and back out onto Sara's street.

"Okay, okay. What *do* you want to do?" she asks.

I pull out onto the main road, thinking. "Want to get a custard?" I finally ask. Frozen custard always cheers me up. And the family-run frozen custard stand up the road has the seasonal pumpkin-pie custard right now—my favorite.

"Yeah, I can go for custard. Let's do it."

A few minutes later I park the car in the gravel lot near the stand. I pull on my navy wool hat and gloves since it's a bit nippy outside tonight. Plus they look cute with my lightweight green sweater. The weather in central Illinois in September is odd—it can be warm during the day but chilly at night. Sara tosses her flower onto the dashboard, then takes her multicolored striped hat out of her pocket and pulls it on.

The custard stand is hopping so we get in line first for our custard and then find a spot at the end of one of the long wooden picnic tables. There is a group of sophomore girls from school at the end of the table and a family with young kids a couple of seats down from us.

Sara takes a big bite of her custard and points her spoon at me. "So spill. What's with the mood? Is cousin-poo driving you nuts already?"

I sigh. "No. Not exactly," I say, and take a bite of my custard, relishing the creamy deliciousness of it.

"Did you see Danny looking at her? Seriously, I was about to stick a bowl under his chin to catch the drool," Sara says.

"Sara! He wasn't drooling over her." I add, "Not really."

"Uh, okay. If you say so. Is that why you're in a mood? You've had four years to ask him out." She stabs at her custard with her spoon.

I know Sara thinks I'm a wimp for not "going for it" with Danny. She has no problem walking up to a cute guy she likes and asking him to a movie or out for a burger. But that's so not me. I'm not the forward type. I'm much more the sit back, smile pleasantly, and pray that he someday, somehow notices me type.

"No, that's not bothering me," I say. "And Milan would never go for him anyway even if he did like her. Which he *doesn't*. He's one of us. He's 'you people.'"

"Huh?" She raises one eyebrow at me.

I quickly fill Sara in on how Milan's been acting since she got here and how she basically thinks we're a town full of a bunch of freaks or something.

"I say ignore her," Sara concludes when I've finished. "Act like she doesn't even exist." She gets up from the bench and tosses her empty custard cup into a nearby trash can.

"I can't ignore her," I say. "She's living in my house—at least for the next six weeks. It's not that big a place, you know. Our rooms are across the hall. We'll see each other all the time. Not to mention she's going to be working at the Patch too."

Sara laughs, sitting back down again. "Yeah, right. Milan Woods is going to do physical labor? I'd love to see that."

"Well, you'll get your chance. She starts tomorrow." I crumple up my napkin and toss it into my empty cup.

"What is Milan doing visiting right now anyway?" Sara asks. "Doesn't she go to school?"

"Mom says she's on some kind of break," I reply.

"In mid-September? Who gets a break in mid-September?"

I shrug. "It *is* kinda weird." Especially during pumpkin season. I mean, we're a pumpkin patch; this is our busiest time of the year. She could have come in winter or spring when we're less busy. In the winter Dad hauls in fresh-cut Christmas trees from a tree farm to sell and Mom sews and teaches quilting classes. And they attend a lot of trade shows in the spring. It's pretty quiet then. But come June, Dad starts planting the pumpkins and Mom is superbusy with all the marketing and getting the shops and stands ready. Then September hits and it's nonstop pumpkinmania, seven days a week.

"Listen," Sara begins. "She's still thinking she's a Hollywood princess or whatever and that we all care who her mommy and daddy are. When she sees that nobody does and she's no better than the rest of us, she'll come down from her high horse. Wait and see." Sara nods matter-of-factly, and I want to believe her.

"I hope you're right. I was sort of thinking that with Milan being here I'd get to see what it was like to have a sister," I admit.

"Hey!" Sara says, feigning insult. "You've got me."

"I know, I know. I mean a live-in sister. True, I haven't seen Milan in years, but she was so much fun back then and I figured we could pick up where we left off. I guess that was a stupid thought," I say, and rest my chin on my hand.

"You haven't talked to her at all since you were six? Haven't you e-mailed? Written letters? Birthday cards? Facebook? Anything?" Sara asks.

I twist my lips. "No . . . not really. I mean, Mom has written and called to talk to Aunt Annabelle and Uncle Jack and she's told us about them over the years. But as for me and Milan specifically speaking? No. Though I did try to add her as a friend on Facebook once. She ignored the request."

Sara smirks. "Well, what was so fun about her back then?"

I cross my arms. "I don't know. Nothing. Everything. We got into a lot of trouble together actually. Like, when we were out in California visiting we went to the beach for the day. Aunt Annabelle was walking down the beach a ways and Milan and I were building this awesome sand castle near my parents. It had at least a dozen turrets. Anyway, Aunt Annabelle suddenly came running toward us with this *thing* in her hand. It looked like a clear, half-deflated water balloon. She was laughing so hard and yelling, 'My plant fell out! My plant fell out!' Well, Milan and I had no clue what the heck she was talking about, but the adults burst out laughing. So we did too. I mean, Aunt Annabelle looked so darn goofy hopping around that way. But then she screamed and we got spooked for a second. We figured it was still part of the joke though so Milan and I resumed laughing. Then Uncle Jack got up and peed on her hand! Right there in front of everyone! So we laughed even harder. And Milan got up and started jumping around yelling, 'My plant! Ah! My plant! Ah!' It was hysterical. The adults were not amused. We had a time-out on Milan's beach towel for half an hour after that. Turned out that thing Aunt Annabelle picked up was a jellyfish that had stung her and the pee was supposed to help relieve the pain. But how were we supposed to know that? I was a pretty good kid, you know, but I had five more time-outs with Milan over that vacation. She was so, so funny. I didn't even mind getting in trouble."

"Aw, that's a cute story. Kind of weird, but fun—aha!" Sara slaps the picnic table and chuckles. "Wait, I just got the joke!"

"What?"

"Your aunt's joke! I bet she said 'My implant fell out!' You know those saline bags they use for boob jobs? I can see how one of those might look like a jellyfish."

I smile. "Hey, yeah, that is pretty funny. I wonder if Milan ever got her mom's joke?" I stop smiling. "I'd tell her but she'd probably roll her eyes at me and call me 'you people' again."

Sara frowns. I can tell she feels bad for me.

I shake my head. "No. You know what? We got off on the wrong foot. Stuff like this probably happens all the time when you haven't seen someone in so long. You can't always have an instant reconnection like on those mushy gushy find-your-lost-relative reality shows. It'll just take us some time. I'll get her to like me yet." I nod, determined.

"Well, whatever. But don't stress over it." Sara stands and tugs at my arm. "Come on, forget about her for now. I know what will cheer you up."

"What?"

Sara grins. "Let's talk about Pumpkin Princess and how *you* are a shoo-in for it at this year's pumpkin festival!"

3

I still remember the first time I understood what a Pumpkin Princess was. I was sitting between Chester and Leroy, two of the goats in the petting zoo, brushing their coats and watching the Patch parade. The parade always starts at the far end of the Patch, taking a route through the Patch and onto the main drag in town. A big crowd had turned out, lining the way with their lawn chairs. There were people carrying orange and green balloons, local farmers driving big green John Deere tractors, the high school band dressed in costumes and playing fun songs, dancing scarecrows, and a giant float in the shape of an ear of corn, carrying people who threw candy corn to the parade watchers. The thing I couldn't take my eyes off of though was the red hay wagon with the corn-husk throne and the Pumpkin Princess sitting atop it.

It was beautiful.

Shelly Larson, Miss Shelly to me back then, was the Pumpkin Princess that year. She was a senior in high school and about the nicest grownup I'd ever met. She had short bobbed brown hair, huge green eyes, and a warm smile. She volunteered at the town library after school and man, could she do a good story time. She also worked at the Patch. She gave tours of the pumpkin farm to the Boy and Girl Scout troops and worked in the craft tent. She often let me hang around with her and be her assistant. She even made me a special braided necklace with a clay pumpkin dangling from it and called it my assistant badge. I wore that thing everywhere.

The day I saw Miss Shelly sitting up there on her throne, with the green rhinestone stem firmly in place atop her head, I knew that someday that would be me too. I could be Pumpkin Princess. After that I wandered the pumpkin fields daily, finding broken-off pumpkin stems in the dirt. I would carefully untie the ribbon Mom had put in my hair each morning and retie it to fasten the broken stem onto my head. I practiced walking up and down the pumpkin rows, waving and pretending that I was Pumpkin Princess.

If I didn't think someone might see me and that people would talk, I'd probably still practice walking and waving in the pumpkin fields. Instead, whenever I get the chance, I head to the red barn way at the back of the Patch. That's where we store the throne. It's also where we store the huge apple-picking baskets, my excuse for coming back here now.

I check around to see if anyone is watching before I enter the barn and zero in on the throne. It's in the far corner underneath a pile of thick wool blankets. I pull off the blankets and examine it. It's huge and amazing. My mom and her friends made it years ago. They spent weekend after weekend twisting and braiding corn husks together and then shellacked the whole thing within an inch of its life. It's really cool and at the end of the parade young kids always want to climb up into it and get their picture taken with the Pumpkin Princess.

I take a seat in it and smooth my hands over the shiny armrests. It's still early and the Patch is pretty quiet. I don't hear anyone nearby. This barn is set far back from the booths so not many people would come all the way out here anyway. It's safe to take a minibreak. I close my eyes and, for probably the thousandth time, envision myself in the parade. I can see the younger kids smiling and waving at me as the tractor pulls the wagon holding me through the Patch. Sara's clapping and hooting and being typically obnoxious but supportive. And there's my mom and dad with their arms around each other, looking proud and telling people around them "That's our daughter." And Danny. He's sitting back a bit from the parade crowd, hanging off his tractor drinking fruit punch Gatorade. Watching me with a crooked smile. I wave to him and he winks. The tractor parks and I start to get down. Danny jogs over and holds his arms up to me, ready to put them around my waist and lift me to the ground. I reach toward his shoulders and . . .

"Jamie!"

Ah! Dad!

I jump off the throne, hurl the blankets over it, and race for the front of the barn just as he's opening the door.

He examines the barn, looking over the baskets and plows and extra shovels and rakes, probably trying to see if anything is out of place. "What are you doing?" His voice has a hint of accusation in it.

I hoist up one of the large red baskets. "Getting ready to pick apples," I say as innocently as I can. "We need some fresh ones up at the farm stand." We do let people pick their own apples of course, but some don't like to do the actual work and prefer to buy a five-pound bag at the farm stand. I drag an arm across my forehead. Man, it's hot in the barn. And not just because Dad's yelling at me. It's gotta be in the 70s this morning. Too hot for September, that's for sure.

"Get a move on, then. Afterward, go up front to help your mother in the petting zoo." He turns and leaves the barn.

"Nice chatting with you too," I mumble. I've already been working for two hours and that's the first time Dad even talked to me this morning. We're not a chatty family in the mornings. Well, Dad isn't chatty ever. We all tend to do our thing without talking about it. Although, I wonder, where's Milan? She's supposed to be "working" here now. She could always go help Mom.

Twenty minutes later I've filled my basket with Fuji and Red Delicious and I'm pulling them to the front in an old rusty wagon. I leave the apples with Martha, the woman who runs the farm stand, and check my watch: 9:45. We open in fifteen minutes and there is still no sign of Milan. I know she is a guest in our home but she's here to work for the whole pumpkin season so she should be, well, working. With the rest of us. But it *is* her first day. I bet she's tired from the trip. I know—after I help Mom I'll stop and get Milan a nice strong black coffee from the concession stand and bring it to her.

On my way to help Mom in the petting zoo I stop at the caramel apple stand to visit Sara. She's putting the finishing touches on today's caramel apples. She makes them fresh each day and they taste amazing.

"Mmm, did you make the Jamie Special?" I ask.

"M&M'S, sunflower seeds, and crushed Cheetos?" she says. "Still disgusting, but yes, I surely did."

"You're the best!" I say. "I'll come back at lunchtime for it. Any new combinations today?"

"Yeah, I'm trying a few new ones. I made two with pumpkin seeds and butterscotch chips in caramel, and a couple of s'mores—marshmallow cream dipped in chocolate and graham cracker crumbs. We'll see if they sell." She shrugs like it's no big deal but the caramel apples are a *huge* deal to Sara. She labors over each concoction, trying to make each new recipe more interesting than the last. And she keeps close tabs on what her customers like and tries to improve on it. Caramel apples are her passion.

I look over the rest of Sara's display. She does carry most of the typical apples you might find at any other caramel apple stand—regular caramel, caramel with nuts, caramel with M&M'S, chocolate drizzle, and so on, each individually wrapped in cellophane and tied with a pretty orange ribbon. But I always look forward to the new ones she comes up with. Like the honey-dipped Granny Smith covered in Gummi-Bears and dried cranberries. It's such a cool talent she has.

"Looking good," Danny's voice says from behind me. I turn to look at him. I wish he was talking about me, but judging by the direction of his gaze he's talking to an apple dipped in peanut butter and pecans.

"Hey, Danny," Sara says.

"Hi," I softly add.

"How are you feeling today?" Danny asks.

"Um, m-me?" I stutter.

"Yeah, you." He grins, adjusting the rim of his baseball cap so he can see me better. "After your Jackie Chan moves jumping off the tower yesterday I was wondering if anything is sore."

I hesitate. Let me see if I can capitalize on his question. If I tell him something is sore, say, my shoulders, for example, maybe he'll rub them? "I'm fine," I reply instead. God, I'm such a wimp.

"Good to hear," he says. He reaches one hand up to his neck and rubs.

"Are you sore?" I ask before I even think about what I'm

saying. Maybe I can rub him? Oh, who am I kidding? I'd pass out before my fingers ever met his neck.

"I think I slept funny or something," he says, still rubbing.

I bet he's beautiful when he sleeps.

"You've got to be kidding me," Sara exclaims, shooting a disgusted look past Danny and me.

My eyes follow her gaze and land squarely on Milan, standing about a hundred yards away, sporting a teeny tiny pink bikini top, the shortest short-shorts I've ever seen, and glittery magenta cowboy boots. The look could easily rival Jessica Simpson's in her *Dukes of Hazzard* days.

"You've got to be kidding me," I echo.

4

I run for Milan, not entirely sure what I'm going to say or do when I finally reach her. My first instinct is to grab one of the horse blankets and throw it over her before my dad sees her out here like this. I don't see any blankets or other alternatives nearby, however. I stop abruptly in front of her, panting. She cocks her head at me, looking slightly amused.

"Um, okay. Hi. Good morning. Hope you slept well and all that stuff," I begin, talking fast. I glance left and right to see if my dad is anywhere in sight. But I don't see him. Yet. "So, listen," I continue. "We don't, um, er, dress like that here at the Patch. Like, we *really* don't dress like that. Not that you look bad or anything, I mean, it's a nice bathing suit and the pink brings out your, uh, makeup. I guess. Obviously you look great, and I'm sure where you're from people dress like that all the time, but seriously, you can't be out here half-naked in front of the customers. If my dad sees you he'll flip his lid. For real," I add for emphasis.

Milan chuckles and shakes her head at me and not in a that-was-a-great-joke-you-told kind of way but in a you-poor-jealous-girl sort of way. But she's got me all wrong. I'm not jealous. Well, not much. I'm not protesting her attire out of envy, but out of a desire to avoid the almost certain confrontation if my dad sees her. I'm looking out for her like any good cousin would.

"I'm not trying to be a prude or anything, Milan," I go on, "but this is a family place. There are kids!" I gesture to a five-year-old boy peeking out from behind a tall corn-husk decoration to emphasize my point. The boy is staring at Milan like she's a double-dipped ice-cream cone.

Milan sighs loudly. "Listen, *cuz*, if I'm stuck out here working all day then I'm going to be working on my tan at the same time." She examines one of her lean arms, admiring her already perfect bronze color.

She's totally trying to brush me off! I can't let her. "Please, Milan. Please go back to the house and grab a shirt at least. The shorts are . . ." I pause, evaluating her way-too-short-and-frayed denim. "Well, they'll do I guess but you really need more on top." I wiggle my index finger in the direction of her over-exposed chest. "And before my dad sees you. Please?" I add, hating how whiny and desperate I sound.

"No," Milan shoots back. "I'm not walking all the way back

to your house just to get a silly shirt. These are new boots and I'm not going to get a blister because you're afraid of a little skin." She reaches down to wipe away an invisible speck of dirt from her right boot and gives Junior a real eyeful of her cleavage. His mother sees him gawking and puts a hand over his eyes.

Argh! I want to pull my hair out. She's so darn frustrating. I'm not afraid of a little skin. It's not like I don't have skin too. My skin is fine. I just don't show it to the whole blasted world. And who told her to wear new boots to work? Okay. Deep breath. It's not her fault. She doesn't know any better. It's like she's from another country or something. Would we yell at someone visiting from England for driving on the wrong side of the road? Okay, we would. Bad example. I need some patience with Milan, that's all. I contemplate making a dash back to the house to grab a shirt for her, to fix the situation, when Danny steps up beside me. Milan straightens like she's noticing him for the very first time and gives him a toothy smile.

Danny's long fingers quickly unbutton the light brown flannel he's wearing. "Here," he says briskly, pulling the shirt off his broad shoulders and handing it to Milan. "Put this on."

Milan looks at Danny, now in only a dark brown tee stretched ever so slightly across his chest, and then at me, and shrugs. While it's a completely logical and utterly sweet gesture on Danny's part, seeing anyone other than myself in Danny's deliciously worn-in flannel will feel like a thousand knife stabs to my heart, I'm quite sure.

Milan takes the shirt, says thank you sweetly to Danny, and slips it over her narrow shoulders.

Yep. My heart is Swiss cheese.

Danny mutters, "No problem," to Milan, and then says, "I better get back to work," to me.

I nod slowly and watch him retreat to his tractor. He needs to get ready to take the first group of patrons on a hayride out to the pumpkin field to find their perfect pumpkins.

When I turn back to Milan she has Danny's flannel sleeves rolled up to Tuesday and she's tying the tails of the shirt up high enough to show maximum tummy.

Of course.

"There. Better?" Milan asks, waiting for my approval.

I try to smile, repeating the Milan-is-new-and-doesn't-know-any-better speech in my head. But all I really want to do is rip Danny's shirt off her and run away screaming "Mine, mine, mine!"

I nod. "Much."

"Good. Then if there's nothing else I'm off to find Uncle Henry and see what it is that I'm supposed to do out here." Milan turns and leaves me.

I stand alone for a moment, watching her, and then head for the petting zoo to help Mom.

"Hey, Mom," I say a few minutes later when I find her with a shovel, cleaning the pony stalls. "I'm here to help."

Mom smiles. "Hi, honey. The ponies still need to be brushed, the pigs need to be fed, and the antibacterial instant hand-sanitizer dispensers need to be refilled. Start wherever."

I nod. It's easy stuff. I grab a big brush and set to work on Brownie, my favorite of the ponies. She's a favorite with the kids too. She's super gentle. "Hey, sweetie," I coo to the pony. "How are you today? Did you miss me?" Brownie grins at me—well, I like to think she's grinning at me—and I rub her nose. She loves Jolly Ranchers and I reach into my back pocket for the three watermelon-flavored ones I brought for her.

"Is Milan out here?" Mom calls to me from the stall she's working in.

"Yeah. Finally," I mumble.

"Dad has her helping Martha this morning," Mom goes on. I can hear her scraping the floor of the stall with the shovel.

"Doing what?" I ask. Martha always has the farm stand in tip-top shape. She never needs help from anyone.

"I'm not entirely sure," Mom says. "But Martha will find something for her to do."

Hmph. So that's how it's going to be this season. Milan isn't actually going to be doing any real work, but rather playing the part of someone working at a pumpkin patch. Nice. I shake my head in disgust and keep working on Brownie's coat.

"You know, Jamie," Mom says in an accusatory tone, "it wouldn't kill you to go out of your way to be nice to your cousin. It's hard living in a new place where you don't know anyone."

"What? I've been nice," I protest. And I have. She's the one who has been cold to me since the second she got here.

"Well, be nicer," Mom says, and turns her back to me.

I sigh. I suppose Mom's right. Milan's barely been here a day. I need to try harder. I'm sure by this time next week we'll be just like sisters. "Yes, Mom." I start brushing Brownie's coat again, then stop. "Hey, Mom," I say. "Why is Milan here, again?"

"I told you. She's on a break."

"But who gets a break a few weeks into school starting?" I press on.

"Jamie . . ." Mom says in that warning tone that means I'm to stop pushing her. She leaves the petting zoo, ending the conversation.

5

When I'm done working for the day, I head for the house, wiping the dirt off the front of my overalls as I walk. I saw Milan leave the Patch over an hour ago and I'm wondering how her first day went.

I greet Mom and head for Milan's bedroom, determined to be pleasant and to try to strike up a conversation with her. I peer in and see Milan struggling with a giant, heavy-looking trunk. It must have been delivered today since she didn't have it with her when she arrived yesterday. I pause, figuring out what I'm going to say. I've got to try again with Milan. We have to get to a good place or these six weeks are going to be miserable. I'm going to kill her with kindness, as they say. I take a deep breath. Okay, I'm going in.

"Hey, Milan!" I sing out cheerily. I stretch my cheeks into such an enormous smile that it almost hurts.

Milan glances over her shoulder at me and then returns her gaze to her trunk. "Hey," she replies flatly.

I rock on my heels, waiting for her to say something else. But she doesn't. Okay. "So," I try, "got more stuff today, huh?"

"Nope. Not a thing."

I give her a quizzical look. Oh. Sarcasm. Fun! Ignore, ignore, ignore.

I step farther into the room and reach out to touch the trunk. "Your luggage is gorgeous," I say, admiring the smooth brown leather with the funny gold letters on it.

Milan sighs heavily and looks at me, no expression on her face.

"You've got to be so tired from your first full day on the Patch. Would you like me to help you?" I offer.

Milan considers this briefly and then pushes back from the trunk. "Yeah, sure. Knock yourself out." She grabs a magazine from the dresser and plops onto the bed. "Oh, wait," she says, lowering the magazine, "can you go wash your hands first? I don't want grub all over my clothes."

"Um, sure," I say, and head for the bathroom. Grub? Baby steps, I tell myself.

I return a moment later. Milan doesn't stop reading her magazine to acknowledge that I'm back, so I set to work. I grab a stack of hangers from the closet and kneel beside the trunk. It's crammed full of expensive-looking clothes. I pull out a couple of plain white tees and feel minorly better about Milan. Maybe she is a normal girl after all. Then I catch the price tag on one of the shirts: $89.99. You've got to be kidding me. I rub the fabric and turn the shirt over a couple of times in my hands. It feels like a normal cotton tee to me. Size xs. No special design, no pocket, no fancy stitching. I don't get it. What makes it so expensive? I want to ask Milan, but I'm sure she'll roll her eyes at me so I put the tees on hangers and walk over to her closet to hang them.

I reach into the trunk and pull out a big stack of tiny, and I do mean *tiny*, denim shorts. They're a rectangular shape and I'm betting if I ran a stitch along the bottom, cut out the middle, and added a zipper to the top they could double for my third-grade pencil case. I don't know how she gets into these things. I fold the shorts, which takes barely seconds, walk to the dresser, and load them into the middle drawer. I look over at Milan and she's concentrating heavily on her magazine. I'll admit this is a little bit weird. I thought unpacking would be something we could do together. Some girl-bonding time.

I pick up a strapless pink floral sundress and hold it in front of me, not sure how to get it on the hanger. "This is cute," I say, hoping to start a dialogue with Milan.

Milan looks at the dress and then back at her magazine. "You couldn't wear it. Your shoulders are much too muscular. Kind of manly, if you ask me."

I stare at her, my jaw dropped. Did she just call me a man? Feeling wounded, I don't reply, but keep making trips back and forth from the trunk to the closet, hanging clothes.

When I'm done hanging Milan's outfits, all thirty-two of them, I perch on the end of her bed, hoping for a nice chat.

Milan senses that I'm not leaving and lowers her magazine. "Yes?"

I stumble with my words. "Um . . ." I'm so not used to this much rudeness! People do not behave this way in Average. "So, uh, tell me about Los Angeles," I finally get out.

"It's hot," she says matter-of-factly.

Okay. "Um, what do you do with your friends for fun there?" I ask.

Milan rubs her forehead with her right hand, like she's getting a migraine or something. "You know," she says, "I'm tired. So if you wouldn't mind." She waves toward the door for me to go, and puts the magazine back up in front of her face.

That's it? Not even a thank-you? I hesitate, trying to digest what just happened, and then rise off the bed to leave. I linger at the door for a moment and look at Milan. I don't understand my cousin.

Twenty minutes later, while I'm in my room writing in my journal, I hear a car pull up outside. I look out the window and see two girls in the front seats. If I'm not mistaken it's Kettle Corn Girl and Sno-Cone Sammy. Both are seasonal workers at the Patch and community college students. I'm not too friendly with either girl. A no-longer-tired Milan runs out the front door, laughing, and jumps into the backseat of the car. I watch the three girls pull away.

I guess it isn't *all* Average people Milan dislikes. Just me.

6

It's midmorning Sunday and I'm getting a little hungry. I couldn't eat breakfast earlier, which never ever happens. I love food. And I'm not tired from staying up too late; I didn't even go out last night. I'm just down. Milan hurt my feelings yesterday. What have I done to her? I'd come right out and ask her why she doesn't like me if I didn't think she'd laugh like crazy at me. I head for Sara's stand for a quick check-in.

"Hi, Jamie!" Molly Jenkins calls as I pass the front of the corn maze. Molly runs it. She takes the tickets and lets people in and if they can't find their way out she goes on in and finds them. She's so sweet.

"Hey, Molly," I say, pausing to chat. "How's it going?"

"Great!" She smiles brightly. "Jacob lost two teeth this morning and Amber started walking last week." Molly's been working here to help her mom out since last pumpkin season, when her dad went on disability. She's got a mess of brothers and sisters and when she's not here she's usually watching them.

"Aw, they're so adorable," I say, and she nods. "Well, you have a good day." I wave and continue on toward Sara.

"Is it getting hotter and hotter today or what?" I ask when I reach her stand.

"Tell me about it," she replies. "Need a water?" She reaches down into the cooler and pulls out an icy-cold bottle of water for me.

"Thanks," I tell her, and rub the bottle across my forehead. "Can I get some M&M'S?"

"Are your hands clean?" She looks down at my hands and I do too. They're a bit dusty but not bad.

"Fairly," I say.

She smiles and scoops a spoonful of M&M'S into a napkin and hands it to me.

I look around the Patch. "Seen Milan lately?" I ask. I heard her come in late last night so I wonder if she's even come out to work today. I focus on my candy, separating the orange M&M'S from the rest on my napkin. I always eat the orange ones first.

Sara nods and chuckles. "That girl," she says. "She certainly stirs things up, doesn't she?"

"What now?" I ask, not sure I want to know.

"Well, let's see. I think she worked with Martha for all of five minutes this morning before Christy and Dana ran over with refreshments."

Christy and Dana work at the main concession stand on the weekends.

"But Milan doesn't eat anything," I say.

Sara's eyes widen. "Oh yeah, I'm pretty sure she told them that because they turned right back around and five minutes later returned with a bottle of water and baked pumpkin seeds."

I shake my head. "That girl," I say, repeating Sara.

"Wait," Sara says. She puts a hand on my shoulder and nods straight ahead. "Here she comes. Watch how the employees look at her."

I lean an elbow on Sara's counter and watch Milan cross from the farm stand to the row of pumpkin weigh stations. My eyes dart around, from the zoo to the pony rides to the craft tent, and sure enough, all the Patch workers have paused in what they're doing and are watching Milan. She's like a traveling car crash. "I don't get it," I say to Sara. "Are you and I the only ones resistant to her spell?"

"It would seem so," Sara agrees, and returns to packaging finished caramel apples.

It's amazing, I think. Just amazing how one girl creates such a commotion. I glance at the entrance to the Patch and see my favorite family, the Spinellis, walking in near the giant pumpkin tower. "Be back in a bit," I say to Sara, and then wave and jog over to the Spinellis. "Hi, Chastity! Hi, Christian!" I say, bending down to hug the six-year-old twins.

"Hi, Jamie," they say in unison, giggling. Christian pulls Chastity's hair and Chastity gives him a hard shove.

"Stop it!" he yells.

"You started it!" she returns.

"No, you did!" he says.

"Need help picking out your pumpkins?" I ask, trying to distract them from annoying each other any further. Plus, I help them pick out the perfect pumpkins every season so it's a tradition.

The kids bob their heads up and down in excitement.

"Well, okay," I start.

Chastity points over my shoulder. "I want *her* to help me. She's pretty!" she says.

Do I even need to turn around? I sigh and look over my shoulder. Yep. Exactly what I thought. Milan is standing a few feet behind me, smiling down at the kids.

"She's busy," I say to Chastity. "I can help you though, just like I do every year."

"Oh, I'm not too busy," Milan says. "And not to toot my own horn, but I have amazing taste in picking out everything from the perfect top to the perfect clutch so I don't think outfitting this sweet little family with the perfect pumpkins will be difficult."

"Yay!" the twins yell, jumping up and down, clapping their hands. Chastity gives Christian a hard shove and he stumbles into me.

"Whoa, careful," I say, straightening him back up.

"She pushed me," Christian says.

"Did not!" Chastity returns.

I try to smile at them but it's hard. I'm not even feeling irritated with Milan's abrupt intrusion, though I know I should be. No, I'm feeling something else right now. I'm feeling hurt that even the kids are choosing Milan over me. And a little jealous.

"I'm supposed to be helping with the pony rides, but you can do that for me while I help the kids. Right, Jamie?" Milan says. She doesn't even wait for an answer. "Let's go, guys." She wraps an arm around the shoulders of each kid and guides them away from me.

Okay. Now I'm irritated. I turn to leave and see Danny standing about fifteen feet away. He must have seen and heard everything. I feel my cheeks go red with embarrassment. I look down at the ground and quickly pass by Danny, not saying a word.

The day can't end fast enough for me, which is a first. Generally I adore my job here. I'd rather be out here than back at the house on almost any given day. I love the Patch. I just never imagined it would be this difficult working with Milan.

7

Milan has only been here a little more than a week and I've had it. For real. I need to get far, far away from her or I'm gonna lose my mind.

I walk in through the back door of the one-hundred-year-old farmhouse, now the number-one scariest haunted house in all of Average and possibly the county. When my parents first bought the Patch they built a new house so we never actually lived in the farmhouse. But when I was little I used it as a sort of playhouse until Dad decided to turn it into a haunted house. I feel my way in the dark until I get to the casket room. There are three black old-fashioned caskets in a row and every thirty seconds a light flashes and Petey Johnson pops out of the middle casket in a Dracula mask. I stand at the bottom of the casket waiting.

"Raaaah!" Petey screams, both hands in a booga-booga wave over his head.

"Hey, Petey," I say.

Petey puts his hands down. "Oh, hey, Jamie. What up?"

"Break time," I answer.

"Cool," he replies. He climbs out of the casket, pulls his mask off his head, and hands it to me. "Back in fifteen."

"Take your time," I say. Really. I'm in no hurry.

I climb into the casket and pull the sweaty plastic mask over my head. This part is kind of gross, but Petey is a fairly clean kid so I don't think he's going to transfer any icky germs to me or anything. That's the hope anyway.

I lay my head down on the cranberry-colored velvet pillow in the casket, closing the top over me, and enjoying the pitch-black darkness. There is nothing to do but lie here until the tiny red signal above flashes, alerting me to jump out. Nothing to do but obsess over Milan and how I'm going to deal with her. I'm not sure I'll be able to make it through pumpkin season with the way things are going now. This is certainly nothing like I'd imagined her visit would be.

"Raaaah!" I scream, and jump out of the casket. No one was even walking through the room to catch my scream. I lie back down and get comfy on the pillow again. There is a faint yet funky smell under the mask today. I'm betting Petey was eating Funyuns earlier. Gross.

I know I shouldn't let Milan get to me like this but it's hard.

Last night I heard Kettle Corn Girl's noisy Audi pull up and the girls were laughing and carrying on as Milan climbed out of the car and came into the house. It was as if she wanted to make sure that I heard her or something. Like a slap in the face—she can hang out with these random unrelated girls, but not with her very own cousin.

And while Milan is completely antisocial to me at the house, it's like she's Miss America out here on the Patch. She strolls from booth to booth visiting with all the employees. I'm surprised she isn't signing autographs. Who am I kidding? She probably *is* signing autographs and I just haven't seen her doing it yet. She's so darn braggy and it's totally getting under my skin. Which is probably exactly what she wants.

"Raaaah!" I yell, popping out of the casket. Two preteens squeal and hug each other and I smile briefly under the mask.

I lie down and stare at the inside of the casket lid. I'm so sick of hearing Milan tell absolutely everyone about her great life back home: how she has one of those giant infinity pools and she swims in it year-round, how designers send her loads of clothes hoping for the chance that she might wear something of theirs out in public and get snapped in a photograph, and how she's BFFs with all these other celebrities' kids, like that wacky Scientologist's kooky offspring. That's not something I'd be bragging about, that's for sure. Everyone else around here is eating it up though. Except for Sara. And Danny doesn't seem too interested, thank God. Of course, the other males at the Patch are panting after Milan like puppies. It's completely disgusting. It's as though they've never seen a pretty girl before.

And she rejects every friendly attempt I make. I even tried to do something I thought she'd want to do. On Thursday night, a rare night that she didn't have plans to go out, I asked her if she wanted to go get manicures and her face lit up. I thought, "Finally, I'm getting through to her! We've found a common ground." Though I've never had a manicure and didn't even know where to go to get one. I never did think much of paying someone to paint my fingernails when they'll just get dirty at work anyway. But I was willing.

So I asked around the Patch and everyone said take her to Betty Sue's. When we arrived at Betty Sue's house she led us to her basement, where she has a sink and a table set up to do nails. Well, Milan. Flipped. Out. She started ranting about nail fungus or cuticle disease or some such thing and stormed out. She acted as if I was trying to kill her by taking her there. Which is ridiculous. Who ever heard of death by nail polish? I was so embarrassed.

Sara thinks I need to stop trying. That I'm only hitting my head up against a wall when it comes to Milan. Mom always says there is good in everyone, but maybe there isn't any in Milan. My feelings haven't been this hurt since third grade, when Susie Schulman had a slumber party and invited all the girls in class minus me.

"Raaaah," I say, more than yell, this time. Hmph. That was pretty pathetic. I don't think I'd scare a kitten with that.

I lie back down and snuggle into the pillow as best as I can. I'm going to clear my mind. A little meditation wouldn't hurt. If I'm thinking about nothing then Milan surely can't upset me.

⌒

"Jamie?" a voice says.

I pop up, ripping the plastic mask off my face. I blink, adjusting my eyes to the dark. Oh, it's Petey. I must have fallen asleep. My power nap did me some good though because I'm feeling more refreshed.

I hand him the mask and climb clumsily out of the casket. I exit the haunted house into the bright daylight and rub my eyes. When they adjust I head for the front of the Patch to find Mom and see who I should relieve next.

Mom is talking to Milan near the giant pumpkin chucker, this huge medieval-looking wooden catapult. My dad put it in three years ago and it's one of my very favorite attractions. For five dollars, patrons can chuck a ten-pound pumpkin out into the field at targets. There are things you can win if you hit the various targets, anything from free popcorn at the concession stand to a twenty-five-dollar gift card for Megastore. People love it.

When I approach Mom and Milan I hear Mom telling her what a top-notch job she's been doing at the Patch. It takes all

57

my willpower to resist putting my index finger in my mouth to make the universal gag sign. Mom goes on and tells Milan how impressed she is that Milan got the pumpkin-chucker bin launched and ready to go by herself, and with extra pumpkins lined up and ready too. I look at Milan, waiting for her to tell Mom she didn't do it.

"Thank you, Aunt Julie," Milan says sweetly. She smiles at me over Mom's shoulder.

Liar! I want to scream. She so did not have anything to do with getting the pumpkin chucker ready to go today. I saw Jeff and Teegan hauling the pumpkins to the chucker early this morning. I glare at Milan but she totally ignores me. Not that that's new.

"Jamie," Mom says, like she is just now seeing me standing here. "Milan will need to rehydrate after her hard work. Go ahead and relieve her for break."

Oh? So I should saunter around the Patch batting my eye-lashes and bragging to anyone who might listen? Easy. But I don't say that. I don't say a word. I'm too mad. Mom never seemed overly concerned about me rehydrating and I work hard all the time.

I watch Mom walk back toward the petting zoo area and Milan join Kettle Corn Girl and Sno-Cone Sammy at Sammy's stand. Milan is laughing about something and the three girls turn in my direction and then rehuddle.

Argh! They're *so* obnoxious! Even the most popular and

58

snobby kids at my school don't act this badly. What a bunch of jerks those three are. And is it my imagination or are Kettle Corn Girl's and Sno-Cone Sammy's shorts even shorter today?

At the end of the day, I'm washing my hands in the kitchen sink when Milan walks in carrying a bouquet of fresh-picked pink and purple asters.

"Aunt Julie? Do you have a vase?" she asks.

Mom peeks at Milan over the top of the open refrigerator door. "Oh, aren't those pretty! Yes, I do. Go look in the bottom section of the china cabinet in the dining room. I should have something there that will work," Mom tells her.

Milan gazes down at the bouquet as she passes by me. "Danny is so sweet," she comments.

Danny? Is she implying that he picked those flowers for her? I grimace. Danny doesn't seem like the flower-picking type to me. But maybe around Milan guys do things they wouldn't normally do. Ugh, I can't watch. I pick up my backpack and head for my room until it's time for dinner.

At dinner I purposely don't sit in my usual seat next to Milan's chair. Maybe she'll actually notice and realize that not everyone thinks she's the most special thing ever to set foot on the planet. I take Dad's seat, forcing him and Mom to have to sit on either side of Milan. As Dad approaches the table he comes to an abrupt stop, noticing the seat change. He stands there, staring at me like I've committed some huge sin or something.

"What?" I finally mumble. "The air-conditioning was making me cold."

Dad frowns and takes my seat without a word.

Milan cheerily enters the room and slips into her seat. "Dinner smells great, Aunt Julie," she comments. "This hard work has really been giving me an appetite."

I cross my arms over my chest and slump back in my seat, staring skeptically at Milan. But she doesn't even glance in my direction.

"Thank you, Milan," Mom calls from the kitchen. "I tried something new. I hope you like it."

Hmph. She never hopes I like anything. Of course, there generally isn't much that I don't like.

"Working at the Pumpkin Patch is so much fun. I had no idea I'd enjoy working as much as I do," Milan continues.

Oh puh-lease. What a load of—

Mom sets a big bowl of steamed broccoli on the table in front of Milan.

I frown. That's new. No cheese or crumbled Ritz crackers on the broccoli. Not even a few pats of butter. Are we on a diet or something?

"Well, you're doing a wonderful job. Right, Henry?" Mom asks, placing a hand on Dad's shoulder.

Dad wipes some milk off his mouth and clears his throat. "Excellent. Better than workers that have been here two, even three seasons."

My elbows drop on the table with a thump. What's this? Compliments from the man who on most days won't even utter a hello to his only child? Is Dad feeling okay? Is there a carbon monoxide leak in the house or something and he's tripping? Milan doesn't even do 10 percent of the work I do around here every day. I never get praise.

Mom sets a big bowl of homemade applesauce on the table and retreats to the kitchen, smiling.

"Gee, thanks, Uncle Henry," Milan says, glancing my way to make sure I'm taking this in. "This looks delicious." Milan scoops some applesauce out of the bowl. She briefly passes it by her nose before dropping it onto her plate. Probably trying to see if Mom put any sugar in it.

Mom returns and sets a big platter of . . . something . . . in the center of the table and takes a seat. She looks proud. It looks like some sort of rubbery ball of meat. And it smells sort of like turkey, but it sure doesn't look like any turkey I've ever seen.

"Tofurkey!" Milan exclaims, clapping her hands together.

Tofurkey? Hehe. Okay, this is going to be good. I look at Dad, waiting for him to give Mom hell for putting a big peachy tofu ball on the dinner table. And I wait. But he doesn't say anything. I widen my eyes at him. Hello? It's *fake meat*. Say something.

"Looks good," Dad says.

8

It's six in the morning and I'm ready for school. I set my heavy backpack by the front door, grab an apple and a banana from the kitchen, and head outside to feed the bunnies before I leave. I eat my banana in three bites, before I'm even at the end of the gravel driveway, and start in on my apple.

I crack open the heavy wooden gate and let myself into the bunny pen. We have a good fifty-plus bunnies of all colors hopping around. It's hard to ever be in a bad mood when you're around these supercuties. My favorites are the gray ones with black spots. We have four of them and they are totally adorable. They are the only ones I've named—Lily, Delilah, Anastasia, and Gwendolyn. I know, I know, it's not Flopsy and Mopsy but these gals seem to fit their names.

"Hello, sweeties! Who's hungry?" I pull down a big bucket of rabbit food from a shelf and give it a shake. But none of the bunnies are paying attention to me. Huh. I shake the food harder. "C'mon, guys!" I call, but the bunnies still pay no attention to me. You know, I'm going to develop quite the complex if even the animals start ignoring me. I look at their water system and see that it's full. That's weird. Somebody has already been in here and fed my bunnies.

I walk to the edge of the bunny hill area and look around the Patch. Who else is out here at this hour?

Suddenly it becomes clear. I spot Mom and Milan walking together in the distance, each carrying one side of a bale of hay, laughing at something. I squat on a nearby step stool and wrap my arms around my knees. I'm hoping Milan didn't see me. That would make her day, I'm sure.

And why is that anyway? I rack my brain, trying to remember if I did something to annoy Milan and make her hate me so much. But no, I've been nothing but nice to her since the second she arrived. I'd like me if I were her. But for some reason she seems determined to make me look bad, not only in front of my parents but also in front of my friends at the Patch. I don't get it.

I look down and Gwendolyn is nibbling at my right shoe like she's hungry. I reach into the rabbit feed, pull out a handful of pellets, and offer them to Gwendolyn. She eats from my hand, watching me. It's pity eating. Like when you're at your grandma's house and you force down a piece of lemon poppyseed cake not because you actually want to, but because it would make Grandma happy.

And it works. I smile at Gwendolyn and rub her back. "Thanks, sweetie."

After the much-needed quiet time with the bunnies, I grab my backpack from the house and jump in my car, purposely not saying goodbye to anyone before I head to school. I'm not sure this was even noticed. No one is paying attention to me these days. I turn on the car radio and crank up the music, trying to drown out my thoughts. Of course, this has never exactly worked for me. I must be a loud thinker. On the one hand, it'll be nice to not be in Milan's presence for a few hours. On the other hand, if I'm away from the Patch, how can I keep an eye on her? What if she takes advantage of my absence to suck up to my parents even more? Or worse, what if she spends the whole day hitting on Danny?

Ugh. It's totally not fair that I have to be in school, worrying about what Milan's up to when all she has to do is homeschool for two hours a day on her pink laptop in her room. She probably won't even do that. She'll bat her eyelashes at some Patch worker and have him or her writing essays for her in a snap.

"Morning, Jamie," Dilly says, slipping into the desk next to me in math class.

"Hi, Dilly," I reply. "Did your hair again, huh?"

Dilly smiles and tucks a piece of hair behind her ear. "Yeah, you like?"

64

Dilly's dark brown hair is newly highlighted with thick Crayola-yellow stripes. "It's totally you," I say. And actually, it's kind of cute.

Dilly looks thrilled. "Thanks! I'm making a statement. It's supposed to be a message to all of the sheepeople out there with their matching haircuts and highlights."

I smile. I've never colored or highlighted my hair so I'm not sure I get the message she says she's putting out there, but I get Dilly. And this is totally her.

"So, how was your weekend?" Dilly asks. She flips open a notebook on her desk and pulls a pencil out of the backpack hanging off the back of her chair. "Did your cousin start playing nice? Did you guys have fun?"

"Fun?" I repeat. Hmm. When I think of Milan the word "fun" doesn't spring to mind. Manipulative, snotty, unfriendly, high maintenance . . . Now those words seem more on target. "Well, I—" I begin, but am interrupted by our math teacher walking in.

"Okay, people, let's get started right away. Open your books to page 112," Mr. Cranshaw says, flipping on the overhead machine and uncapping a dry-erase marker.

I watch Mr. Cranshaw's scribbled letters and numbers appear on the large screen hanging on the wall at the front of the room and I know I should be taking notes like everyone else in class. But, really, how am I supposed to care about dividing one polynomial by another polynomial when at this very moment Milan could be blowing in Danny's ear? It's driving me crazy not knowing what she's up to back at the Patch.

At lunch I buy a greasy cheeseburger in the school cafeteria and take it outside to eat. I stop in front of a shady apple tree, kick the rotten apples lying on the ground out of the way, and plop down to call Sara. She answers in one ring.

"What's up?" Sara asks.

"Nothing, what's going on there?" I reply. I absentmindedly pick up a red apple lying on the ground nearby and roll it around in my free hand.

"Well, my Peanut Butter Cup apples are selling like crazy."

"No, you know what I mean. What's *she* doing?"

"Who?"

"Sara!" I say, exasperated.

"You mean Precious? She's . . . Well, I believe she thinks she's working. Socializing while doing the least amount of physical exertion is a more accurate description, however," Sara says.

"Is she, I mean, has she been talking to Danny?" I ask, hating how I sound. But I can't get those flowers she brought home Saturday and her implication that they were from Danny out of my mind.

There's a pause.

"Sara?" I prompt, knowing that if it's taking her this long to answer then I'm not going to like what she says. At all.

"Well," she begins, and she pauses. "Here and there. I wouldn't get worked up over it though," she adds quickly.

My heart sinks. Milan is totally blowing in his ear.

Neither of us says anything for a moment. Not that we need to. We're both thinking the same thing.

"Seriously, Jamie," Sara finally says. "I don't think she's Danny's type. Don't worry."

I appreciate Sara's effort to make me feel better, but I'm having a hard time seeing Danny turning Milan down if she is in fact throwing herself at him. "Just, keep an eye on them, okay? And let me know if she's hitting on him."

"All right, I will. But I really do think it's no big deal," Sara adds.

"Thanks," I say, and we hang up.

The rest of the afternoon goes by slowly and I race for my car after the final bell rings. Ever since I hung up with Sara I've been getting these horrible visions of Danny and Milan sneaking off behind one of the barns to make out. I have to get back to the Patch and see for myself what's going on.

When I get home I change into my overalls at warp speed, throw my hair into two braids, and get out to the Patch. I walk from booth to booth, acting like I'm looking for something, but actually I'm trying to find Milan. I finally spot her in the face-painting booth, surrounded by a bunch of preteens, and I breathe a sigh of relief. At least Danny's not with her. I hang back for a moment, studying her. She's smiling and looks like she's having a good time talking to the group of girls. One of them turns around to shout something to her mother and I see exactly what kind of face painting Milan has been doing.

I'm at Milan's side in ten fast steps. "Excuse me," I say to the group of girls, and give Milan's arm a tug.

Milan throws me an annoyed look and snaps her arm free from my grasp. "What?"

I motion to the back of the booth with my head. "Can I talk to you for a moment? Over there."

Milan lets out a loud, dramatic sigh and slowly stands. "I'll be back in a sec," she says to the girls, and they nod eagerly. She drops the makeup tubes and brushes onto the table with a thud.

I wait in the back of the booth and Milan steps in front of me, arms crossed. "What did I do now? Is my outfit offending you today?" she asks.

I briefly glance at her outfit. True, while it's short, tight, and skimpy, at least she's not flashing anything. I shake my head. "No. That's not it. It's only, did anyone tell you how to do the face painting?"

Milan turns her head and looks at the group of girls smiling at her and then returns her gaze to me. "They look good. What's there to tell me?"

"Well." I lower my voice. "You have them done up like Bratz dolls with those big magenta eyelids and lips. And that heavy eyeliner . . . I mean, you're supposed to draw things on their cheeks. You know, like pumpkins and hearts and smiley faces. Haven't you ever had your face painted as a kid?"

Milan looks at me like I'm about the stupidest person to walk the face of the earth. She rubs her lips together and says, "Listen, when you start wearing makeup then maybe I'll consider your advice as to how to apply it. But right now, I don't need any help from *you*." With that, she turns and heads for the waiting girls. "Okay, ladies, where'd we leave off?"

I stare at Milan's back, stunned. I totally *do* wear makeup. I just don't cake it on like Milan does and I certainly don't wear it for work. And the way she said "you" like I'm the worst person ever or something.

I glance around the face-painting booth and see that I've been dismissed by both Milan and the group of girls she's entertaining. And I'm not going to lie, my feelings are hurt. I was only trying to be helpful. She *is* doing it wrong.

I slink out of the booth and walk down the path to the storybook barn. It was always one of my favorite places as a kid. The outside of the barn is painted in a cheery yellow and the inside is full of large panels with various storybook and nursery rhyme scenes painted on them. There's Humpty-Dumpty on one and Little Red Riding Hood on another. Jack and Jill running up the hill, the kid in the corner with the pie, and Mary and her lamb play out across more panels. There is a large bookcase full of children's books, and teeny tiny tables and chairs for the kids to sit and color at if they want while they're listening to the stories. Or they can sit on the big cushy circle carpet. And there is a giant Mother Goose in the middle of the barn that the kids love to climb on and mothers love to snap their pictures with. Maybe I'll find a comfy beanbag and read to some of the little kids for a while. Or hide out.

I stay in the storybook barn for the rest of the afternoon, avoiding Milan. I read Dr. Seuss, Eric Carle, Shel Silverstein, and Kevin Henkes to the kids. And I do feel a bit better. You can't be in too foul a mood after reading *Lilly's Purple Plastic Purse* three times. When it's close to dinnertime I start walking toward the house and spot Milan talking to Danny, while he's unhitching the hay wagon from his tractor. I stop and watch them, which is probably not the best idea in the world. But I'm dying to know what they're talking about. Milan glances in my direction and then I see her point down at her feet and then point at the tractor. It looks like she's wearing heels. Really, really high heels. Like the kind women only put on to pose for a picture in a magazine and not to actually walk in. When did she even put those on? She wasn't wearing them in the face-painting booth. And who in her right mind wears heels to work in a pumpkin patch anyway? Danny shrugs and nods and next thing I know Milan is standing up on the back of his tractor, holding on to his shoulders. She smiles at me as they roll away.

I feel like someone punched me in the gut.

9

I gently push open the front door of the house, trying not to let it creak and alert the family that I'm home.

"Jamie, is that you?" Mom calls from the kitchen.

Darn it. Man, she's got good ears. I fling the door open the rest of the way and step inside. "Yeah," I say reluctantly.

"Great. Can you set the table for dinner, please?"

I sigh. What, no "How was school today, Jamie? How did work go, Jamie? Anything new in your life, my dear sweet only child?" I trudge into the kitchen and fling open the cabinet door where the dishes are. I pull down four plates and reach for the silverware drawer with my free hand. Mom is rushing around the kitchen, pulling things out of drawers.

"Oh, hon," Mom says, "grab an extra setting, would you? Milan invited a friend over for dinner."

"What? She did? Who?" I fire off. Oh my God. Not Danny,

not Danny, not Danny, I chant in my head. Anyone but Danny. If I have to sit here and witness a family dinner date between Milan and Danny I'll die.

"That nice girl Samantha from the Patch," Mom says, wiping up a mess on the counter with a handful of paper towels.

"Sno-Cone Sammy?" I practically yell. My moment of enormous relief is quickly replaced by annoyance that I will soon be sitting across from one of Milan's drones. One that doesn't seem to exactly like me either.

"What did you call her?" Mom says, pulling a loaf of homemade Italian bread from the oven and setting it on the counter to cool. She looks at me quizzically, waiting for an answer.

I turn away, reaching up into the cabinet for another plate. "Um, nothing. I didn't realize that Milan was having a friend over or I would have asked Sara to come too."

Mom crosses in front of me to the refrigerator and pulls out a couple of pears, a tub of crumbled Gorgonzola cheese, and a bottle of cranberry vinaigrette. "Another time, Jamie," she says, not looking at me. She places the ingredients on the counter next to a couple of heads of romaine lettuce and a bag of walnuts, and pulls down a large salad bowl from one of the cabinets.

I nod and start to leave the kitchen. Whatever is in the oven smells good. "What's for dinner anyway?" I ask Mom.

Mom's face lights up. "A vegetable frittata," she replies. "You'll love it."

"Oh." I try to smile like this sounds like a good thing. I head for the dining room table and on the way out spot the empty white plastic bag on top of the garbage. Blech. More tofu.

I stare at the two empty seats across from me at the dinner table. Mom clears her throat for the second time and Dad is sitting with his arms crossed, watching the food in the middle of the table get cold.

"Can I have a piece of bread?" I ask.

"In a minute," Mom returns quickly. She twists the napkin in her hand over and over again. It looks like a fat white worm.

"Dinner looks wonderful, Aunt Julie."

We all look up at the same time and see Milan and Sno-Cone Sammy have finally graced us with their presence.

"Thank you, Milan." Mom has a huge smile on her face. "Come, sit down." She drops the napkin and pats Milan's spot at the table.

I notice Milan and Sno-Cone Sammy are wearing similar plaid belted tops and dark leggings. Funny how Milan won't wear a plaid shirt out to the Patch to work, but she'll iron one, dress it up with chunky rings and bangles, and wear it to dinner.

"I hope we didn't take too long. We didn't want to come to dinner in our work clothes," Milan says, taking her seat. The girls both laugh and Milan's eyes land squarely on me.

Whatever. I've been coming to dinner in my work clothes ever since I first started working at the Patch. I reach out for the bread bowl and throw a couple of pieces on my plate. I scoop a massive hunk of spreadable butter out of the container to my right and smear it on one of my pieces of bread. I look right at Milan and take a big bite. It's like I'm saying "You may be fooling people with this act of yours, but I'm going to eat carbs *and* fat. So there."

I chew. And chew. And you know, it's kind of a disgusting amount of butter for one bite. But I'm no quitter. I take another bite. Milan raises an eyebrow in my direction and drops some lettuce leaves onto her plate, careful to avoid any of the yummy stuff Mom put in the salad. Okay, so maybe my eating a scoop of butter with a smidge of bread isn't effective revenge on anyone but myself.

This is going to be a fun dinner, I can tell.

Milan and Sno-Cone Sammy are carrying the conversation, talking about how skinny Hollywood is these days and the unhealthy message it sends today's youth. Which is ironic since I've probably eaten more in one sitting than Milan has eaten since she moved in with us. Dad's keeping his gaze downward, concentrating heavily on his dinner. Mom keeps looking back and forth between everyone at the table, trying to gauge how we're enjoying the food. And I've got a huge, barely touched piece of vegetable frittata sitting on my plate. I can't eat it. Not because it's tofu. I'm too mad to eat. And, well, my stomach hurts a bit from all that butter I inhaled.

"It was such a fabulous idea bringing Milan to work here at

the Patch, Mr. Edwards," Sno-Cone says. She squeezes a piece of lemon into her iced tea and stirs it with a spoon.

Dad looks up at her and does this nod/grunt thing and then returns his gaze to his plate.

"Really," she continues. "Milan has some fantastic ideas for the Patch. I think they can make you *a lot* of money."

At the word "money" Dad's ears perk up and he looks at Milan. "Really, Milan?" Dad says. He throws a napkin on his plate, giving up on the rest of his dinner. "Like what?"

"Well," Milan begins. She sits up straighter in her seat, clearly happy to have attention on her. "For starters, I think we should sell a homemade pumpkin facial scrub in the gift shop. Pumpkin facials are all the rage back home. They're fantastic for your skin—especially this time of the year, when people tend to have a lot of dead skin on their face." She pauses and looks at me.

I touch my cheek with my hand. I so do not have dead skin! I scowl at Milan.

"Anyway," she continues, "pumpkins have this enzyme in them that totally attacks the dead skin cells. Not to mention, there's loads of zinc and vitamins A and C that totally brighten the complexion. And the scrub smells amazing. Seriously, it'll fly off the shelves if we stock it." She looks at my dad expectantly. She's so darn sure of herself.

My dad leans back in his chair, considering this. After a few seconds he looks at Milan and gives her a huge smile. And my mom smiles at my dad. Everyone looks happy. Except for me. I cross my arms and slump in my seat.

"Good thinking, Milan," Dad says. "We can probably do that. What do you say, Julie?"

Mom's nodding. "It sounds like a great idea. I'm sure I can whip it up. And we can put it in tiny adorable jars. You'll help me make it, won't you, Milan?"

"Of course," Milan agrees. "I'd love to!"

What? Are they joking? She's been here for all of a week and a half and now we're letting her develop products?

"It'll be a lot of fun," Milan continues. "And Jamie can fetch us the pumpkins. Right, Jamie?"

Everyone looks at me. I give them a tight smile. Yay. I can be the pumpkin fetcher. Wonderful.

"Tell him your other idea, Milan," Sno-Cone urges.

Oh God, there's more?

Mom and Dad look at Milan eagerly and Milan is grinning. "Okay. You know how you sell hot chocolate and hot apple cider at the concession stand?" she asks. "I think you need to sell something else for more"—she waves a hand in the air—"sophisticated tastes."

Dad gives Mom a puzzled look. I know what he's thinking. Sophisticated and Average aren't exactly synonymous. "What do you suggest?" he asks.

"Pumpkin spice lattes," she returns, clearly pleased with herself.

I'm secretly pleased too—Dad's going to shoot this idea down. He hates froufrou coffee drinks. Straight black coffee is all he sells at the concession stand.

Dad twists up his face. "Hmm. I'm not sure about that one, Milan. It sounds a little . . . complicated."

"Oh, but it's not, Uncle Henry," Milan says. "I've been working the espresso machine at home since I was six. If you get an espresso machine for the concession stand I'd be happy to make the pumpkin spice lattes."

Dad mulls it over for a few moments and then finally grins. "Okay then. I guess it wouldn't hurt to give it a try. Let's do it."

And that's my signal. I abruptly stand. "May I be excused?" I say to Mom. "I have a lot of homework tonight." That, and I can't sit here and listen to this for another single second.

Mom nods. I pick up my plate and utensils and head for the kitchen, pausing briefly at the garbage can to dump in my dinner. I place my dishes in the sink and head for my bedroom, avoiding the dining room.

Once I'm safe behind my bedroom door, I fling myself onto my bed and let out a scream into my pillow. I flip over onto my back and whip my pillow across the room, almost knocking over my desk lamp. I'm *so* mad! What the heck was that? Now Dad's kissing Milan's butt too? C'mon!

I get off my bed and pace around the room. It's ridiculous. This whole thing is completely ridiculous. You know, I've always told myself that Dad couldn't help being so cold to me.

That he always wanted a boy and did his best dealing with the disappointment of my being a girl. But with how he's acting with Milan now, well, he's never been nice to me like he is to her. And she knows it. So let's get this straight—not only is Milan seeking Danny's attention, now she wants my Dad all to herself too?

I kick my thick history book lying on the floor and let out a yelp. "Ouch, ouch, ouch," I whisper, sitting back on the bed and leaning over to rub my toe. Ugh. That's going to leave a bruise.

I need to zone out, to forget things for a bit. Maybe read a book or watch TV. I glance at my nightstand and spot the Pumpkin Princess registration form. Hmm. I'll work on that for a while. Maybe that'll take my mind off Milan.

Question #1: Why do you want to be Pumpkin Princess?

That's easy. I smile and begin writing.

10

Well?" I whisper into the phone. I lean out from my hiding spot and scan the hallway for teachers or administrators. I've ducked down between a row of lockers and a giant garbage can.

"Jamie?" Sara says.

"Yeah," I reply anxiously. "You know it's me. What's going on?"

"Dude, you need to relax! This is the fourth time you've called today. Aren't you supposed to be in class?"

I know Sara is losing patience with me. I've driven her nuts this week calling so much to see what's going on with Milan and Danny. But I can't help it! I know Milan's up to no-good. I need to get through one more full day of school and then I can keep an eye on her myself.

I check the hallway again. Still clear. Though I'm sure I

don't have much time. "Yes, yes. Of course. But it's only gym and I got a pass to the nurse's office to get a Band-Aid."

"You're bleeding?" Sara screeches. "Jamie, go get your Band-Aid and we'll talk after school. I can't believe you're calling me while you're injured."

I look down at my index finger wrapped in Kleenex. The cut is tiny and my finger is hardly bleeding. I know I'll survive a quick phone call. "Sara, please tell me. I can't stand not knowing what's going on there—with *her* and Danny—while I'm stuck at school. Just tell me. Is it bad?" I hold my breath, waiting.

There is silence. "Um..." Sara finally says.

My breath comes out in a whoosh. "Oh God, it's bad. It's bad!" I repeat. Oh, I knew it! Sara is trying to spare my feelings. It's awful.

"I didn't say that," Sara says. "All I said was um. 'Um' is a filler word used when one wants to gather his or her thoughts and—"

"Sara!" I interrupt.

"Okay, okay," she relents. "But it isn't *that* bad."

"Tell me." I dig the fingernails of my phone-free hand into my knee.

"Well, they had lunch together. On the hayrack," Sara says.

"What? They did? No one else was there?" I ask, feeling slightly hysterical. I peek around to see if anyone can hear me. There is a janitor pushing a big broom down the hall, but he's not paying any attention to me.

"No," she says slowly. "It seemed to be, well, one might think that it possibly could have maybe looked . . . a little like a date."

"What?" I scream.

"I could be wrong, I could be wrong!" Sara interjects. "It's not like she and I are best buddies and she told me this. We don't ever even talk. It's only that I saw her carry a picnic basket over to him and then they both climbed up on the hayrack."

"Kill me now," I say.

"Come on, Jamie, it might be nothing. It doesn't mean he likes her. She probably cornered him and forced him to have lunch with her."

"Right," I say dryly. "I can hear him now. 'No, no, stop coming on to me, beautiful, rich daughter of famous movie stars. I'm saving myself for the girl in the pumpkin-smeared overalls with dirt under her nails.'"

"Jamie . . ." Sara says quietly.

"It's fine," I reply quickly. "I'm fine. Listen, I've got to get back to class before someone finds me out here on the phone. I'll see you after school."

I hit End on my cell and check my finger. It has stopped bleeding already. Guess I don't need that Band-Aid now.

I pull myself up from the floor and start walking slowly back toward the gym, almost running head-on into Dilly.

"Hey, Jamie," she says. "I was just coming to look for you. Ms. Grenovich was worried that you were passed out from blood loss somewhere between the gym and the nurse's office."

I try to grin. "Nah, I'm fine. It already stopped bleeding." I wave my finger at her.

Dilly frowns. "You look upset."

"Oh, I'll be fine." I shrug.

"Do you want to talk? We can break out of here and go sit at the Burger King," she suggests. Burger King is the only fast-food restaurant in all of Average so it's not like we'd exactly be inconspicuous sitting there in the middle of the school day.

"We'd better not," I say. "We're in our gym clothes." I point to our matching yellow tees and maroon shorts. "We'd totally stick out and I don't want to get in trouble. Let's go back to class."

We return to gym and join the class in playing floor hockey. Floor hockey always gets a little aggressive—it's like a free pass to chuck people you don't like in the ankle with a wooden stick. Not that I think anyone would try to hit me, but I like to stay out of the cross fire so I keep some distance between me and the puck. Dilly and I hover near the goal, talking. I tell her how Milan is only getting worse and that I don't know how I'll survive the remaining four weeks of pumpkin season living with her.

"Well," Dilly says after I finish telling her about Milan and Danny's lunch date, "I don't know your cousin, but I do know you, and you rock."

My cheeks pink at the compliment.

"She must have some serious issues to be harassing you like this," Dilly continues. "I wouldn't take it personally. And this thing with Danny? If he's smart he'll avoid the chick with the issues. I think guys can sense that kind of thing. Let her go on making a fool of herself and she'll eventually get a clue." Dilly seems so sure.

"Really? I mean, you think Danny might avoid her?" I ask hopefully.

"Oh sure," she concludes, like it's the most obvious thing in the world. "You know, I'm a pretty good judge of people. I think I'll stop at the Patch and pick out my pumpkin today, and, you know, check out the situation."

My eyes widen. "You're not going to say anything, are you?"

"Of course not. Just picking out my pumpkin." She grins.

"In that case, I'll give you a ride over after school," I offer.

"Deal."

The last bell rings and I see Dilly leaning on the passenger door of my car in the student parking lot.

"Ready to pick out your pumpkin?" I ask when I reach her.

"Definitely," she says. "This year I'm thinking of going for a big, round, fat one. At least a forty-pounder."

"Sounds good," I reply. I unlock the car and we get in.

We park near my house and walk to the Patch, heading for Sara's caramel apple stand first. I have to say, Dilly has made me feel a lot better about the situation. I mean, it kinda makes sense that there is something wrong with Milan and not with me.

"Hey, Sara," I say when we reach the stand.

"Hey, Jamie. Hi, Dilly," she replies. Sara and Dilly have met a couple of times before but we haven't actually ever hung out together.

"What're you working on?" I ask Sara, pointing to the paper on the table under her forearm.

She looks at the pen in her hand and the paper, surprised. "Oh, this? Nothing." She quickly folds the paper and jams it into her back pocket.

"Come on, tell me," I plead. "What is it?"

Sara shakes her head. "You'll laugh."

"No, I won't," I insist. "Promise."

"Well..." Sara pulls the paper back out and smooths it out on the table. "It's an application. For school."

"Oh, Sara," I exclaim, "that's fantastic!" I lean over the stand and give her a hug, excited that she's decided to give school a second chance. "Why on earth would I laugh at that?"

"It's for a cooking school. You know, like, for desserts and stuff," she adds.

"That's cool," Dilly says.

"It *is* cool! That's so perfect for you, Sara," I say. "But do we have a cooking school in Average?"

Sara twists up her face. "No. It's in the city. I'll have to move there if I go. At least for the school year."

My stomach drops. "You're leaving?" Sara can't leave. I'd be lost without her.

"Not yet," she says quickly. "I'll be here for the entire

pumpkin season. If I get in I'll start after Christmas. In the winter quarter."

"Oh." While I'm happy that she's not leaving right away I still can't imagine not seeing her every day.

"Don't be sad. It'll be good. Think of the yummy stuff I'll be able to bake for you when I come home for visits." Sara looks happy. She must really want this.

I try to smile. "I know. It's only that I'll miss you."

"I'll miss you too," Sara says, and reaches over the stand to give me another hug.

Dilly coughs uncomfortably.

"Sorry, Dilly," I say, pulling away from Sara.

" 'S okay," Dilly says.

"She's picking out her pumpkin today," I explain to Sara. "I'm going to help her." I turn to go.

"Cool," Sara says. "But wait—before you go. There's something else."

I look back. "Yeah?"

Sara hesitates. "Well, brace yourself."

Oh no. I throw a look at Dilly, my heart racing in anticipation of whatever Sara is going to say. "Braced," I say, though really I feel like I could drop into a puddle at any moment.

"You know I'm friends with Kate, right?" Sara starts. She turns to Dilly to explain. "She's one of the cookie bakers. She works days." Sara returns her gaze to me. "Well, Kate is friends with Laurel." She pauses to address Dilly again. "Laurel is the funnel cake maker here, and also Mayor Hudson's wife."

"Yeah, I know Laurel," Dilly says. "She's on the town board with my mom."

Sara smiles. "Oh yeah, that's her. Okay"—Sara puts a hand on my forearm and takes a deep breath—"well, Laurel told Kate who told me that the townspeople on the Pumpkin Princess committee are strongly urging Milan to run for Pumpkin Princess."

"What?" I take a step back. I can't believe it. I must have heard wrong. It's completely absurd.

"Pumpkin Princess," Sara repeats. "They want Milan to run. They're probably doing it to make her feel welcome. Or maybe they think it will be good publicity for the town, like if it leaks out to one of the big newspapers . . ."

I can't hear her anymore though. I can't hear anything. It's like someone pressed a Mute button on the world. I'm numb.

This girl has come to my town and turned my life upside down. She wants everything I have—my family, my friends, and now she wants to be Pumpkin Princess too.

I look at Dilly. Her face is a mix of concern and sympathy. She's saying something. I try to focus in and listen.

"It's okay, Jamie. I'll try to find out what's going on. I'll ask my mom," Dilly says, trying to comfort me.

"Hey, Dilly," I reply. "You know that something-wrong-with-Milan theory? I know the something wrong. She's *evil*."

11

It took me the rest of the afternoon to calm down. Sara made me my favorite caramel apple, heavy on the M&M'S. And Dilly hung out with me at the pumpkin chucker while I chucked pumpkins at targets, pretending they were Milan. She's lucky she wasn't anywhere in sight because I'm pretty good at pumpkin chucking and I hit enough targets to win three bags of apples, two free popcorns, a twenty-five-dollar gift card to Megastore, and a large pumpkin spice latte. I didn't collect any of my prizes though because technically family can't win at any of the games at the Patch. But you know what I would have done with that pumpkin spice latte? Milan would have been wearing it.

I drop Dilly off at her house and head home. She was reluctant to let me go—I could tell she was worried that I would go home and really chuck something at Milan's head across the dinner table, but I assured her that I was okay. A few minutes later I pull up in my driveway and turn the car off. The front lights are on and I can hear laughter inside. I take my time walking into the house, unsure of what I'm going to do or say, if anything, to Milan when I see her.

"Jamie, where've you been?" Mom says, cranking her head around to look at me. She's sitting at the dining room table, holding an almost empty dish of her Pumpkin Surprise. She invented this concoction when Milan moved in. It's only pumpkin puree and fat-free Cool Whip. That's it. No sugar or spice or anything. The surprise is that anyone actually eats it. "You missed dinner," she adds, stating the obvious. Dad doesn't even look up from his dessert. He keeps spooning in bite after bite. He's eating so fast I doubt he's even tasting it. Which is probably a good thing.

I don't answer Mom though. My eyes are glued to Milan's. "Is it true?" I finally ask.

Milan gives me her extremely annoying smug smile. "Is what true?"

"You know what I'm talking about," I answer, my voice steady.

"Can't say I do," she quips. "You really outdid yourself, Aunt Julie. This is absolutely delicious," Milan tells Mom, ignoring me.

"Pumpkin Princess. Are you running for Pumpkin Princess?" I press on.

Mom clasps her hands together. "Oh, what a lovely idea."

I break my stare with Milan to scowl at my mom. Traitor.

I grasp the back of my empty chair tightly with both hands to keep steady. I can feel anger welling up inside me. "Are you or aren't you? It's a simple question."

Milan puts a bite of Pumpkin Surprise in her mouth, chews, and swallows. "That little contest you guys have going on around here?" she says, waving her spoon in the air. "In two weeks, right? Yeah, I think I did agree to do that."

"Little contest? *Little contest?* That you call it a little contest is exactly why you shouldn't be in it!" I practically spit at her.

"Jamie . . ." Mom says warningly. She slams her spoon down on the table for emphasis.

"What?" I yell at Mom. "She doesn't even know what it is."

"Yeah, but it's sounding more and more interesting every moment," Milan says, smirking at me.

"And why is that? Huh? What is the real reason you're running for Pumpkin Princess? Go on, tell everyone."

"That's enough, Jamie," Mom interjects. "You're being very rude. I think it's a wonderful idea for Milan to participate in the town festivities."

I glare at my mom. Who is this woman and why has she turned on me? I try to steady my voice, realizing Milan is only enjoying my hysterics. "But Mom, she's not even from Average. She can't represent our town, our pumpkin patch . . ."

"Well, actually," Dad says, and we all look at him, startled that he's getting involved in this conversation. "Milan has been a great help at the Patch since she arrived. I think she has as good a chance as anyone to be Pumpkin Princess."

I feel like I've been slapped in the face. I can't believe my dad is defending her too. They're both on her side. It's like, erase one daughter, insert a new one. I can't take it. I run from the dining room straight into my bedroom and slam the door as hard as I can. I press my back against the door and slide down to the floor. And I cry long and hard, like I haven't cried since I was seven years old and got lost at the tractor show. Then, like now, I was completely and totally alone.

I wake up half an hour later than usual this morning and my eyes are raw and puffy from last night. I jump in the shower and get ready for school and though I should be feeling really crappy from last night, I'm actually feeling slightly better. Not great— I mean, my family basically ditched me on the side of the road like an unwanted barn cat. But I'm feeling better about Pumpkin Princess. Who cares if Milan runs? It's not like she'll ever win. It isn't Mom or Dad or Sno-Cone Sammy or Kettle Corn Girl who gets to choose Pumpkin Princess. It's the town. Milan is only a visitor here—she doesn't have the long-standing following that I do in the community. No one with any sense would vote for her over me. It would be absurd.

Of course, that doesn't mean I'm going to be nice to her. Oh no, not one bit. Nice Jamie is taking a vacation where Milan is concerned. I open the refrigerator door and grab a couple of apples to take with me for breakfast. I spot Milan's quart of soy milk on the top shelf and accidentally pour the entire thing down the sink. Whoops. Hope that doesn't wreck her high-fiber cereal this morning.

Okay, so maybe ruining her breakfast is minor league, but being mean doesn't come to me as naturally as it does to Milan. But I'm learning. I grab my stuff and leave for school.

I make it through the day without calling Sara for one single update on Milan and Danny, and I'm quite proud of myself. Of course, I don't know how long I'll be able to hold out. It's like sitting next to a giant bowl of raw cookie dough and not dipping your finger into it for a taste. In other words, practically impossible. But I try hard to distract myself whenever thoughts of Danny and Milan together creep into my mind.

When I get home from school, I park my car at the side of the house and run in to get changed. The house is quiet so I assume that everyone is still out at the Patch working. There is a cinnamon-apple smell in the air, but I'm thinking it's more the air-freshener type of smell than the yummy dessert kind. I'm antsy to get out on the Patch and get to work. I want to remind people how necessary I am to the Patch, and how hard I work around here. I want people to automatically think Pumpkin Princess when they see me.

I walk briskly toward the field where we grow the squash and gourds. I pass Sara on the way, but don't stop to chat, only wave and smile. I need to put in extra effort while I'm working today. And that means I have no time for snacks and chatting.

I arrive at the stand set up at the front of the field and relieve Jake from his post.

"Hey, Jamie," Jake says. "Do you need to borrow my gloves?" he asks, looking at my gloveless hands.

Shoot. I was so anxious to get out here that I forgot to grab my work gloves. I eye the small group of patrons waiting for me to take them through the field to pick squash and gourds. Jake's gloves are enormous and my hands would swim in them. But it's not like I can run all the way back to the house to get mine either. "No thanks, Jake," I say with a smile.

He shrugs as if to say suit yourself and begins walking back toward the front of the Patch.

"Ready to go?" I ask the waiting group, and get several head bobs in return. "Let's do it, then," I say cheerily. I grab the large wagon full of cardboard boxes waiting to be filled and lead the group out into the squash field. People love picking out their own squash and we grow just about every type of squash imaginable: spaghetti, acorn, butternut, banana, carnival, buttercup, delicata, Hubbard, and, well, the list goes on and on. The thing people don't love so much? Actually *picking* the squash. These buggers have got to be the most prickliest vegetables ever. Customers tend to just point at which squash they want and I do the picking. And on any normal work-glove-wearing day I can't say that I mind.

I load box after box of squashes and gourds for the

customers and even carry them out to their cars and set them carefully in their trunks, never letting on for a second that my arms are on fire. I'm dying to run back to the house and run my arms under cold water and then dip them into a vat of cortisone. But not until I've finished my shift. I've got to be at my best.

I'm loading a box of gourds into the back of an old Cadillac when I see Milan sashay by me, chatting with a couple of cute guys, probably in their early twenties. Milan's shorts are hiked so far up today that they look like underwear that's a size or two too small. I ignore her though, and ask Mrs. Mackinski, the Cadillac owner, if there is anything else I can do for her.

"No, no, thank you, dear," she says. "But you should do something for your poor arms, sweetie." She points at my red bumpy skin.

"Thanks, I will," I reply, trying not to scratch at my arms. Her mentioning them alone makes me want to itch them even more. I rub them together for a second to relieve the itching, but then stop right away. I know if I get started scratching I won't be able to stop.

Milan doubles back and flings her head at me. "Ew, Jamie. What did you do to your arms? They're so gross!"

"Why, thank you, Milan," I reply in a voice as icy as the Arctic. At least I hope it is. "But *I'm* working. What are you doing?"

Milan's eyebrows shoot up in an innocent look. "I'm working too," she claims. She flicks her head to the right so that her hair swooshes behind her. The guys seem to appreciate this.

"Doing what?" I return.

She juts both of her palms toward me, each one filled with a tiny orange miniature pumpkin. "I'm carrying these guys' pumpkins to their car." She glances back at the guys, who are both staring at her butt.

I roll my eyes and turn away from Milan. How ridiculous. Those pumpkins can't be more than two pounds apiece. Max. That girl . . .

I feel myself start to rage inside but I stop. No, I'm not going to let her get at me. That's exactly what she wants.

I face her again. "Wow, Milan, impressive! I didn't know you'd moved up to carrying two miniature pumpkins. Soon you'll be able to do three. Keep up the good work!" The snarkiness flies from my mouth before I can stop it. Shoot. That was harsh. Not that I think anything I could ever say or do could hurt Milan's feelings, but I don't want to look like a horrible person in front of people in our community.

I tell Mrs. Mackinski to have a good day and then head back to the squashes.

"Ahhh, yes! Oh my God, that feels *so* good!" I cry.

"Dude, I don't know why you did this to yourself," Sara says, shaking her head. She pulls the plastic cover off a second tube of cortisone and squirts a giant glob on my right arm. She spreads the cream down my forearm and I thunk my forehead on the kitchen table, finally feeling relief from my crazy-itchy skin. "You know you're supposed to wear gloves."

"I know, I know," I say, sitting up. "I was being stupid." Stupidly trying to prove myself, I should say. I don't know why. Nowhere in the Pumpkin Princess description does it say one needs to torture oneself picking squash with bare skin. It's only that I didn't want to make all those people wait for me to walk to the house and back. People hate waiting. Next time I'll have to remember my gloves.

I lean back in my chair, examining my white gooey arms. They are feeling much better, but I hope they'll look better soon too. I've never gotten such a bad rash from picking squash.

"Where is everyone tonight anyway?" Sara asks. She leans out of the kitchen and peeks down the hall. Sara would never admit it but I think she's a little scared of my dad. She doesn't like to be at my house when he's home. It doesn't help that he's always scowling at everyone I bring here.

"Mom and Dad went to some meeting in town and Milan is out with Kettle Corn Girl and Sno-Cone Sammy," I reply.

Sara giggles. "Oh yeah, her 'entourage.'" Sara leans back on a stool and absentmindedly flips through a *People* magazine on the kitchen counter.

"Her entrée-what?" Leave it to Milan to go and get one of whatever Sara is talking about.

"You know, entourage. Her people. Her caretakers. Like Britney Spears has—or, what's her name? You know, that chick who's famous just for being famous? Anyway, they're the people that go everywhere with her and remind her that she *is* as cool and as pretty as she thinks she is. And of course in Milan's case anyway, it means they're going to do her hair and makeup for the Pumpkin Princess competition. You know, entourage," Sara concludes. She pulls a low-fat whole-wheat pretzel out of a bag on the counter and stares at it skeptically for a moment before taking a bite.

I instantly feel annoyed but I'm not sure why. "Whatever," I say. "It's not like you need an entourage to win Pumpkin Princess. I can do that stuff myself."

"Hey," Sara says, like she just got a great idea. "I can be your entourage! It'll be fun. And maybe Dilly can help too. We can do your hair and makeup and help you get dressed backstage."

A tiny smile escapes me. Well, even though it's completely unnecessary it might be kind of fun to have my own entourage. "Okay," I say to Sara.

She smiles and I feel a tiny pang. I'm going to miss her when she goes away to school.

"Ooh, and I know exactly where to start," Sara says. "Did you see that great-looking new pumpkin facial stuff in the gift shop? I can pick up some and—"

"Don't you dare," I interrupt. "That stuff doesn't come near my skin," I add.

Sara gives me a funny look and shrugs. "Okay. No facials. Noted."

12

I love shopping on Saturday afternoons," Dilly announces.

I close my eyes and give the earring spinner I'm looking at a whirl, kinda like a roulette wheel. Maybe I'll land on something good. I grab a plastic earring holder off a hook and look at it. Hmm. Giant neon-pink hoops. Nope, not a winner this time.

"Why?" Sara asks.

Dilly picks up a loud purple plaid golf hat and pulls it on her head. She examines herself in the mirror on the sunglasses spinner. "Because the moms and their little boogers are off at soccer games and birthday parties. There are usually only teens in the stores."

I glance around the Megastore. It's surprisingly bare of kids.

"Yeah, you're right. So, what are we looking for today?" Sara asks me.

"Do you still need a dress?" Dilly adds.

I shake my head. "I have a dress already." Actually, I've had it for almost a year. I found it on sale online late last fall after season and I couldn't resist buying it early. It's been hanging in a garment bag in the back of my closet all this time.

"What? Why haven't you shown me?" Sara asks.

"I haven't shown anyone yet. But you'll see it soon enough," I say. I don't want to tell her that I'm sort of shy about the dress. It's pretty fancy, and a long, long way from my typical overalls. "Anyway, I was thinking of getting some lipstick or something."

"Wait, I'm doing your makeup," Sara says. "But we probably should check colors on you."

Dilly holds up a box of hair color. "What about your hair? Want me to dye it?"

Flashes of bright colors race through my mind. I'm definitely not ready for that big a change. "Um, no thanks."

"Over here," Sara calls from a few aisles over. "There are samples."

"Ooh, I love samples," Dilly says, and tugs my arm to follow her.

Sara and Dilly comb through the samples, discussing colors, and I take a seat on the bottom shelf of the endcap, resting my head on my knees.

"What's wrong?" Sara asks, looking down at me.

I sigh. "I don't know. I was thinking, what if Milan actually wins Pumpkin Princess? That's going to suck so bad."

"Oh, she won't. You can't think like that," Sara says.

"Yeah, but what if she *does*? I can hope and hope that everyone will vote for me. That they will think I'm the right person for the job. But what if they get caught up in the Milan craze and forget about me?"

"Hmm." Sara looks stumped.

A few seconds later Dilly speaks up. "Maybe you should campaign?"

"Campaign? No, I couldn't do that. That would be tacky," I argue.

"It's not a bad idea," Sara says slowly. "It might help to remind people that you're here and running for Pumpkin Princess too."

I shake my head no but now I'm thinking about it. Maybe I could. But only if I'm subtle.

❧

I've been thinking about it since our shopping trip on Saturday and I've decided that I *will* campaign. But only a little. Starting today, as soon as I get out of my school clothes and into my work clothes.

I head out to the information table near the entrance. Today I'm supposed to be demonstrating and giving tips on good pumpkin-carving techniques.

I grab the stem of the big pumpkin on the table and hold a knife in my free hand. "You know how when you make the opening at the top of the pumpkin?" I ask the crowd of ten or so patrons, watching me get ready to carve the pumpkin. "Well, sometimes it takes a bit of time to line it back up when you put the top on. One thing you can do is leave a small notch—in this case I'm going to make a one-inch triangle here at the back of my opening. Now, see how when I want to put the top back on I match up the triangles and I don't have to mess around with it."

"Ahh," a couple of the women say. I see Milan join the crowd and watch me. But I ignore her.

"I actually learned this tip from Gabby Ranebaker. Remember—the Pumpkin Princess from three years ago? She also worked at the Patch back then. Like me." There. That's pretty subtle. "I think it's good to have a Pumpkin Princess who's a hard worker, and especially someone from the Patch, don't you think?" I ask no one in particular, hoping I'm not laying it on too thick.

"Speaking of hard workers," Milan interrupts. "Know what that reminds me of? My good friend Anthony Taylor. You know, the YouTube sensation turned platinum recording artist? He's writing a new song called 'Real Hard Worker.'"

"What? He is?" one girl says. "You know Anthony?" another girls asks. "What's he like?" someone says. And off they go, forming a circle around Milan to hear her talk about yet another famous friend and ending my presentation. Grr. She so did that on purpose.

I try again on Wednesday afternoon. And this time I'm going to do less talking and more bribing. I open up the large

Tupperware tray I'm carrying and display the fifty pumpkin truffles dipped in white chocolate that I made last night. It's Mom's old recipe and they took forever to make. But they taste like heaven and people can't resist them. I pass them out to customers one by one. I feel like one of those sample ladies we see at the big warehouse club we go to once or twice a year to stock up on bulk items.

"Want one?" I ask Milan. I know perfectly well that she doesn't, but I don't want to be rude to her in front of all these people.

Milan makes a horrified face. "No, never. Don't you know that corn syrup kills?"

I gape at her. "Wh-what?" Corn syrup so does not kill. And I didn't put any corn syrup in these anyway.

The woman holding a pumpkin truffle midair on the way to her mouth suddenly drops it back on the tray.

Milan smiles. "Here, would you like one of these great iPhone cases I'm passing out today instead?" she asks the woman. Milan pulls something out of a bag I didn't even notice she had swung over her shoulder. It's an iPhone case with a close-up picture of Milan's face on the back and her name written in glitter across the bottom. Gag.

The woman nods and Milan hands her one. "Anyone else?" she asks. "I've got plenty."

I step back and watch people line up for Milan's iPhone cases. I don't get it. I bet half of these people don't even own iPhones. And even if they do, who wants Milan's big ol' head on their phone?

On Thursday, I'm working at the register, weighing and checking out pumpkins, but my mind is elsewhere. The contest is a little over a week away and I'm not sure how to get people to vote for me without coming right out and asking for their votes. And that's tacky. I've thought about buttons and stickers that say "Jamie for Pumpkin Princess" but that's even worse. And even if I came out with something like that, Milan would just do it bigger and better.

Speaking of Milan, she's headed right for me. I'm going to ignore her and concentrate extra hard on weighing these pumpkins for Mrs. Fini and her kids.

"Hi, Jamie," Milan sings out.

I can't help myself; I look up. And the first thing I see is her shirt. "Hey," I yell, "you can't wear that! You didn't win yet!" Milan is wearing a supertight orange T-shirt with the words PUMPKIN PRINCESS bedazzled across her chest.

" 'Yet' being the operative word," she replies.

Ooh. Did I say "yet"?

"And it seems to me that I can wear what I like," she continues. "Don't be so jealous, Jamie. It's not cute. And besides, maybe you'll get runner-up."

I slam one of the Finis' pumpkins down a little too hard on the counter. I am completely and totally 100 percent furious with Milan. Just as I'm about to rip into her I glance up and see Danny watching us from outside the tent. My heart is racing and I take a deep breath, trying to calm down. I hate looking lame in front of Danny. He probably agrees with Milan and thinks I'm jealous too.

I ignore Milan and turn my attention back to Mrs. Fini. "That'll be twenty dollars, even," I say in the steadiest voice I can manage.

13

I'm supposed to pick Sara up in ten minutes to go out but I can't find my hairbrush anywhere. Maybe I left it in the bathroom this morning. As I head down the hallway I hear talking coming from inside Milan's room. I wonder who she has in there. I pause outside her door and listen.

"Oh God, it's dreadful. No joke, Gabrielle," Milan says.

Gabrielle? Who the heck is Gabrielle? I lean in closer to hear better.

"For real," she goes on. "This has got to be the most boring place on earth. There is literally nothing to do. They have one store for the entire town. Can you imagine? And the people, well, you know how midwesterners are." Milan lets out a loud laugh.

How dare she! What does she mean "how midwesterners

are"? How exactly are we? I'm pretty sure friendly, family-oriented, and hardworking isn't what she's implying.

I wait for her to say more, but there's only silence. She must be on her cell phone.

"You're so right," she finally says. "And get this, oh you'll love it, promise. Okay." She pauses. "I'm in a contest." She laughs again. "No, seriously, I am. Swear. It's called Pumpkin Princess."

There is silence. This Gabrielle person must be asking her what Pumpkin Princess is.

"It's so lame, like everything else here," Milan says.

I feel my blood boiling. I knew she wasn't serious about Pumpkin Princess! It's been an act. She's only doing this because she knows that I want it.

"Of course I'll win," she continues. "Please, like there is any competition here. I could walk out there in a garbage bag and win hands down."

I gasp. The nerve!

"And the prize is some silly little beanie or something. I don't know. Samantha says it's actually cute, but I can't imagine how it could be. It's supposedly a pumpkin stem covered in green rhinestones. What? A stem. You know, that curvy thing at the top of the pumpkin? It's like the handle for carrying it. Yeah, that's it. Well, the winner gets to wear this thing on her head. Isn't that the funniest thing you've ever heard?" Milan dissolves into giggles again and I storm back to my room, forgoing the search for the missing hairbrush.

I drop onto my bed and cross my arms over my chest. I'm so mad. This is exactly why Milan shouldn't be within a hundred yards of the Pumpkin Princess contest. How my parents think she'd represent our town adequately is beyond me. I wish they had heard her talking so badly about it just now. They and everyone else around here need to be straightened out on what kind of person Milan really is.

Pumpkin Princess is a cherished tradition in our town. I'm positive people wouldn't vote for Milan if they knew how poorly she thinks of everyone. There has got to be a way I can show people who Milan is without being pegged as jealous and catty. I know that's exactly what Milan will say if I call her right out on what I overheard. Girls with seriously bad attitudes like hers always claim that everyone else is jealous of them. And, sure, that may be the case sometimes. But sometimes the problem is that they are real witches. And it's no use going to Mom and Dad; it's obvious they will take her side over mine. No, I'm going to have to think long and hard about this and figure out a plan that will work. Milan can't be Pumpkin Princess. I can't let it happen.

I finger-comb my hair as best I can and race off for Sara's house. We're already late to meet Dilly at the town hall. Once a month our town puts up a giant movie screen and shows an old movie behind the town hall. There's a big hill right there and just about everyone comes out with their blankets and bags of microwave popcorn to watch the show. The movie is generally not great but it's something different to do. Tonight they're showing the 1989 Michael Keaton version of *Batman*.

"Dilly," I call out in a loud whisper as Sara and I weave in and out of blankets, trying to spot Dilly's. Hers has a giant blue Care Bear with a glow-in-the-dark tummy so it shouldn't be that hard to find. But there are a lot of people and a lot of blankets out here tonight.

"Jamie!" Dilly says, and I whirl around. We passed her. We backtrack two blankets and move up the hill one.

"Hey," I say, taking a seat on her blanket.

Sara drops two bags of popped microwave popcorn and three diet root beers on the blanket before plopping down beside me.

"I was wondering when you guys were going to get here," Dilly says.

Sara looks at me to respond.

"My fault," I say. "I was running late. But with good reason. I was eavesdropping on Milan."

Dilly's eyebrows shoot up in interest.

"Really?" Sara asks. "You didn't mention it on the way here."

A fuzzy static sound comes over the speakers and lights flash on the giant movie screen. They're warming up the projector.

I better make this fast. I quickly relay every single word Milan said to her friend on the phone.

Dilly hugs her knees and rocks back and forth. Sara shakes her head and flings burnt pieces of popcorn out onto the grass while I talk.

"So what do I do?" I ask when I'm finished.

"Hmm. I don't know," Sara says. "But something has to be done or she's going to turn Pumpkin Princess into a big joke."

Dilly nods in agreement. "Yeah, but Jamie's right. She can't call her out. No one will believe her."

We sit quietly, thinking. The opening credits of *Batman* start and a baby cries somewhere up the hill. I turn around to see who it is. The Applegates had their baby a month and a half ago, but I'm not sure they'd bring her out here to a movie in the cool night air like this. I scan the crowd, but don't see where the crying is coming from. My eyes land on someone a heck of a lot more appealing though: Danny. He's a good ten blankets behind me, sitting right on the grass, his long legs stretched out before him. He looks like he's still wearing his jeans and flannel shirt from work. The two guys he's sitting with are tossing popcorn at each other, but Danny's ignoring it. He spots me looking at him and waves. I return the gesture and quickly turn back around. I shudder. I cross my arms and rub them with my hands. Geez, he can give me shivers even when he's a good sixty feet away.

Sara leans in to me and whispers, "The contest is only a week away. If you're going to out Milan to the town, then you're gonna need to find a way to do it without anyone knowing it's you. Something anonymous."

Anonymous. I nod and turn my attention toward the screen.

On Saturday morning, Mom decides we need more decorative gourds at the Patch entrance so of course she asks me to go fetch them. My arms tingle at the mere thought of touching the gourds and squashes again. But I don't have to pick them today. Mom said Jake already put together a box of the best-looking gourds for me. I'm still wearing my work gloves anyway, just in case.

I start the trek to the gourd field, my mind racing. I need to develop a surefire plan to get Milan. Something that will let people see beyond the glamorous Hollywood stories and glittery boots. Something that can't be linked back to me. But what?

I'm so deep in thought on my walk that I don't even notice when I veer off track. Not until I hear Dad's voice. What's he doing out here?

I stop dead in my tracks. About fifty feet away is Dad's giant six-hundred-pound pumpkin, his pride and joy. Every year he grows a giant pumpkin and gets his picture taken in front of it. Seriously, we have an entire album full of just him and his giant pumpkins. And truthfully, the rest of the people in town love seeing Dad's yearly giant pumpkin and getting their pictures taken in front of it too. I can't even tell you how many hours he spends each year picking just the right genetic seed, perfecting the soil mixture, and fertilizing and watering the pumpkin as much as it needs. He's got a passion for it.

Dad's talking to someone on the other side of it. I can hear a female voice, though it's muffled and I can't make out the words. One thing is for certain, it's not Mom since she sent me out here for the gourds.

I crouch down and creep closer to the giant pumpkin, using it as cover. I know there's a bench about twenty feet away on the other side of the pumpkin. Dad put it there in case people wanted to sit and gaze at the pumpkin for a while. I peek around the pumpkin, hoping to eavesdrop on Dad, and my stomach tightens. I recognize that hair and that ensemble. He's sitting there on the bench with Milan. And she's crying.

I jerk back behind the pumpkin and clench my fists. Argh! What is she up to now? And why is she crying to *my* dad?

Did she run out of her favorite shade of lipstick and can't find something similar to it at our sad town store? Or maybe her eyebrows aren't getting the proper attention she feels they deserve, with no eyebrow-artist-to-the-stars here. Obviously she's faking the tears to get my dad's attention. She doesn't have any real problems. A split end is a crisis in her eyes. A dead cellphone battery spells doom. This girl is *unbelievable*.

I peek around the pumpkin again and see Dad put a comforting arm around Milan's shoulders.

I gasp and fall on my butt in the dirt behind the pumpkin.

Dad and Milan stop talking and I'm afraid they heard the thump when I fell. I don't move. A few seconds later they resume talking and I let out the breath I was holding in. My chest is burning and my skin is feeling prickly. I'm dizzy too. God, please don't let me pass out behind Dad's stupid giant pumpkin, I mumble to myself. I put my head down on my knees and take several deep breaths. A few minutes later, when I feel like I can lift my head up, I peek around the pumpkin and see Dad and Milan walking away, back toward the house.

What on earth was that about? Why did he . . . How could he hug her like that? He's never hugged me. Geez, I don't think he's ever even patted me on the back—not even when I made the winning goal in a soccer game when I was ten. I can't remember a single time when he's ever said "I love you." I mean, I've always assumed that he must, because that's what parents do. They love their kids. I thought it was a thing with him—that he didn't show affection to, well, anyone.

But he does show affection, to Milan anyway. I squeeze my eyes shut and rub them with the backs of my hands. This is stupid. I'm not going to cry. I'm not. I have to get out of here. I forget about the gourds Mom asked for and start running, heading for the front of the Patch, intending to pass through the parking lot and hit the road. And from there I'll just have to see how far I can get.

I run past the concession stand, past the storybook barn, and past the bunny hill and petting zoo. I'm running so fast I can feel the dirt kicking up behind me and hitting the backs of my legs. I'm about to pass Sara's booth when she sees me and dashes out from behind the counter, waving her arms in front of her.

"What's wrong?" she says, grabbing both of my shoulders and pulling me to a stop. "Are you okay?"

My heart is beating extra hard in my chest. I stare at the ground with my hands on my hips, trying to catch my breath. I feel my bottom lip start to shake. I don't know what to say that won't make me sound like a whiny baby.

"Jamie? What's going on?" Sara urges, though in a less panicked and more soothing voice now.

The smell of hay is in the air. I turn around and Danny is standing behind me, concern all over his face. Of course. Perfect timing.

"You shot by me like a jackrabbit," he says. "Is something wrong? Are you being chased?"

Oh man, this can't get worse. I can't let Danny see me like this. I give Sara a pleading look. She understands, and nods. "She's fine," she tells Danny over my shoulder. "I'm going to go with her to get some water."

My chest is still heaving and I'm trying to regulate my breathing.

Sara loops her arm through mine and I think we're going to get away when Danny speaks again. "But what were you running from?"

"She wasn't running from anything," Sara responds quickly so that I don't have to. "She's been doing these sprints—gearing up for the track team this year." Sara presses her lips together and nods, affirming her story.

I finally chance looking at Danny. "Yeah. Track," I say, wondering if he's going to buy this excuse.

He considers this for a moment and adjusts the dark baseball cap on his head. "Track, huh? Okay. Well, good luck with that, I guess," he says.

Ugh. I feel bad for lying to him. That's not good. And he really does look concerned about me. It's sweet how he came running over to see what was wrong. No one else did. Except for Sara of course. "I . . ." I begin, not sure where to go from here.

"Let's go get you that water now," Sara says, tugging me away from Danny. I'm kinda glad to follow her since I had no idea what to say to him. She abruptly stops and yells back over her shoulder, "Danny, do me a favor? Get one of the girls from concessions to cover my booth for fifteen, okay?"

"Sure," he replies, and Sara drags me out of there. We don't talk and we don't stop walking until we're out at the pumpkin chucker. It seems I've been spending a lot of time here these days.

"All right," Sara says when we stop walking. "Tell me what's wrong." She crosses her arms over her chest and looks at me with concern.

I shake my head. I can't tell her. I'll sound like a big baby.

My daddy likes Milan more than me, wah, wah, wah. Sure, it's true, but I can't bring myself to say it out loud. And if I can't tell Sara, I obviously can't tell anyone else.

We both stand there, silent. Sara gives me a sad look. I know she wants to cheer me up and I appreciate her caring. But I can't make any words come out. It's too embarrassing.

"Well," she finally says, "if you don't want to talk then let's chuck some pumpkins. You know that always makes you feel better."

I shake my head and plop onto the ground, staring straight ahead. Sara takes a seat next to me. Honestly, the only way the pumpkin chucker is going to make me feel better today is if I strap Milan's skinny butt to it and chuck her toward Los Angeles.

14

When I wake up Sunday morning, I want to get out of the house as soon as possible. It's not comfortable for me anymore, not with Milan here. I'm not talking to her, obviously, and I've been ignoring Mom and Dad. I don't think Dad notices— either that or he doesn't care—but I think Mom knows I'm giving them the cold shoulder. Oh well, I say. They've made their choice crystal clear; they can talk to Milan if they're feeling chatty.

I get in my car and drive to the Burger King to meet Dilly for breakfast. She's a bit of a sausage-biscuit fiend, and I could use the distraction.

I walk into the restaurant and it's pretty full for a Sunday morning. I give a small smile to some neighbors sitting at a table as I scan the room, but I don't see Dilly. Maybe she changed her mind?

"Jamie, over here," a girl with a mass of pink hair the shade of Sweet'n Low packaging calls to me.

"Dilly?" I screech. "Holy smokes, what did you do to your hair?" I walk quickly to her booth and slip in across from her.

She reaches up and pats her hair. "This? I was tired of the highlights and wanted something new. Do you like it?" She smiles, waiting for my response.

She looks like the fluffy pink cotton candy you can get on a stick at carnivals. Or like one of those dolls you win for a quarter if you can pick it up with the big metal-hand grabber. But I would never say either of those things of course.

"Adorable," I reply. And I'm not lying. It *is* adorable, in a Strawberry Shortcake sort of way.

"Here." Dilly pushes a small white paper bag across the table to me. "I got an English muffin with grape jelly for you."

"Aw, thanks, Dill," I say, suddenly feeling ravenous.

"Yeah, I'm a big spender." Dilly grins. "So, how's your weekend been? Are things with Milan getting any better?"

I stick my tongue out and shake my head. "Nah. And they probably won't. Not until she leaves town anyway," I add. I unwrap my English muffin and poke a white knife through the jelly container's plastic lid. I squeeze some jelly on the muffin and start spreading.

"Oh," Dilly says, like she just remembered something. "I did get a chance to talk to my mom about Milan. You know, about the deal with her running for Pumpkin Princess."

I stop spreading. "Yeah?"

Dilly nods. "Sara was right. My mom said it was some committee lady's bright idea to get extra publicity for the festival. She thinks it'll get a few more pictures in some of the nearby newspapers. It's so not a big deal though. My mom says Milan will never win." Dilly takes a sip of her orange juice.

"Really?" I say, hoping I don't sound too eager. But I'm craving reassurance like a sugar addict craves chocolate.

"Yeah, she hasn't even been in town that long," Dilly continues. "It would be completely ridiculous if she won." Dilly crumples up her wrapper and tosses it in her bag.

"That's what I think too," I say quickly.

"My mom thinks you have the best chance. You have the qualities they're looking for," she adds.

"She said that?" I ask. How sweet! That's what I've been hoping this whole time—that people would see I was the right person.

Dilly nods and I'm completely filled with joy. This one conversation with Dilly has me feeling better than I have in days. It's like they always say about good triumphing over evil. I'll come out ahead in the end. I pick up my English muffin and take a big bite. Maybe things aren't as bad as I thought. Maybe I just needed to get away from the Patch to clear my head and really see what is going on.

I head for home, my mood a hundred times better than when I left this morning. I pull on my work clothes and go out to the Patch, excited to tell Sara what Dilly told me about Milan and the Pumpkin Princess committee.

"Morning, Sara," I sing when I reach her booth. "It's finally starting to feel like October, huh?" I say, taking a deep breath of the cool air. This is my absolute favorite weather.

"I know, isn't it great? You're in a good mood today," she comments, studying my face. She picks up a cap off the counter and pops it on her pen.

I smile. "Things feel better today. What are you working on?"

Sara looks down at the white paper bag she was doodling on. She flips it around so I can see. There is an oval with a thick border and inside it are two crisscrossed delicious-looking caramel apples with the words SARA'S SWEET TOOTH written over them in big bold letters.

"Wow!" I exclaim.

Sara looks pleased. "Do you like it? It's the logo for my future sweetshop," she says. "Once I get out of school of course."

"I love it," I say, and I really do. It's so cool seeing Sara go after her dream like this. "Are you going to let me work for you someday?"

"Oh sure, you can be my taste tester."

"I'd love that job!" I say.

Sara laughs. "I know you would." She folds up the paper bag and slips it into her back pocket. She grabs a wet dishrag and begins wiping down the counter.

"So, listen, I just got back from breakfast with Dilly and

she had some interesting things to tell me," I say, excited to relay the news to Sara.

"Oh yeah?"

I quickly fill Sara in on my conversation with Dilly. As I talk I see Sara's face start to fall. Since what I'm saying leans more to the side of a happily-ever-after kind of story and not a tragedy, I'm not getting her reaction.

"What?" I ask, halting my story. "Why do you look like I took your cookies or something?"

"Eh, um, uh," she stammers. "Man. Why do I feel like I'm always the bearer of bad news lately?"

"What bad news?" I ask, frowning. Ugh. And I was so ready to have a good day today.

"Well," Sara begins reluctantly. "Laurel was over here giving me an earful this morning."

That's nothing new. I nod, urging her to continue.

Sara rubs her chin and twists up her face. I can tell she doesn't want to tell me whatever it is she's about to tell me. "She seems to think there is some sort of 'Milan Movement' in the works," she finally says.

"What? What the heck is a Milan Movement? If it has anything to do with moving her back home to California then I'm all for it. Shoot, I'll pack her suitcases myself. I'll order her a plane ticket. I'll even make her a tofu-rice-cake-whatever-it-is-she-likes snack for the plane ride."

Sara sighs. "No, that's not it. I'll just tell you what Laurel told me. Basically, the mayor of Average paid a visit to your dad and told him how he thinks Milan's presence in our town is our 'ticket to fame and fortune,'" Sara says, adding dramatic air quotation marks.

"Fame and fortune?" I repeat, more like a question. "That makes no sense."

"She said the mayor read something about how Forks, Washington, became a big tourist attraction after the Twilight books were published and he thinks if they promote Milan's being here, our little Average, Illinois, will turn into a big tourist attraction too. He told your dad that his Patch business will probably double if not triple. And that all the businesses in town will benefit."

"What? No. This has to be some kind of crazy gossip. It makes absolutely no sense. And besides, if the mayor really came here to talk to my dad, don't you think I'd know about it?" I ask. Of course, I haven't exactly been talking to my parents lately because I've been so mad. But surely I would have heard something about this before now. Maybe.

Sara shrugs helplessly. "I think it might be true," she says in a soft voice.

I lean my elbow on her counter and rub my forehead, waiting for the next hit.

"Your dad came by a little while ago," she finally says. "He told me to create a new caramel apple—a Golden Delicious dipped in organic, fat-free, sugar-free caramel sauce and covered with golden raisins and"—she pauses, trying to read my expression—"he said to call it 'The Milan.'"

"Oh, yuck," I say, totally disgusted, and not because the apple sounds disgusting, though it does, but because my dad is officially naming an apple after her now. He's never done that for anyone. Sure I have an apple, but the Jamie Special has always been something Sara makes for me on the side; it's never been on the menu. But now here is Milan getting her own special apple. I can't stand it!

"There are other changes too, from what I hear," Sara continues. She pulls on the thumb of her left hand with her right index finger, like she's going to tick off a list of items. "Like the pumpkin spreads at the farm stand have new labels with Milan's picture, they're passing out stickers printed with MILAN WOODS PICKED MY PUMPKIN at the checkout, and . . ."

I throw my hands up in the air. I can't hear anymore. I turn and walk away from Sara's caramel apple stand. I hear Sara yell, "Jamie, wait!" But I walk faster.

I'm not working today. I'm going to take a sick day. And you know what? I do feel sick. I can't believe how every last person, well, except Sara and Dilly, but everyone else, has turned on me. Even my town, the town I've known and loved my whole life, is on Milan's side now. Stickers. Hmph. Give me a break! But it's not like there's anything I can do. There are too many people on Team Milan. I'm going home and I'm going to bed. I just plain give up.

Milan and Danny are standing in front of the concession stand, holding bottles of water and talking. I need to walk right by there to get home. The best thing for me to do is move fast without acknowledging either of them. Danny's eyes keep darting to me over Milan's head though and I can see her moving around, trying to block him from looking anywhere else but at her. But unfortunately for her she's not tall enough to obstruct his view. I'm about to pass by when Danny calls out to me.

"Hi, Jamie."

Normally Danny's acknowledging me would make my whole day. Heck, it'd get an entry in my journal, that's for sure. But I can't. I just can't take him and Milan. Together. I give him a quick wave but keep moving. It's like pulling off a Band-Aid—I gotta get out of here fast or it's gonna hurt.

I walk through the front door of the house, pulling out my pigtail holders and running my fingers through my hair as I cross the living room. I want to get out of these clothes, put on my comfy smiley-face PJ pants and tee, and hide under my covers. And God help the first person who offers me a piece of toast with Milan Woods pumpkin spread on it.

I'm almost safely behind my bedroom door when I notice I'm not the only one home.

"Jamie?" Mom calls from the dining room. "Can you come here?"

I stand still. Is she going to yell at me for not working today?

Too bad, because I'm not going back out there. Milan's working anyway and she's such a hard worker and all so they certainly don't need me.

Or maybe she wants to personally tell me about this business with the mayor. Well, too little, too late. I don't want to hear the sordid details. How does she think this is supposed to make me feel? Did any of them, for even one second, take my feelings into consideration? Nothing she says is going to make me feel a bit better so I'm not about to listen. Unless there is a really good reason for it all. Like, Mom and Dad are six months behind on the mortgage payment and about to lose the entire pumpkin patch and they hate having to shove Milan in my and everyone else's face at every turn, but it's the only way they can possibly pull through their financial disaster. If that was the case then I might listen, for like thirty seconds.

Ugh. I trudge to the dining room. Mom is sitting at the table, surrounded by boxes and loads of homemade candles to sell in the craft barn. I keep my mouth tightly sealed, but I raise my eyebrows, waiting for her to talk.

Mom smiles. "Be a dear and drop off this large pumpkin candle in Milan's room, would you, Jamie? She loves the scent."

Argh!

No explanation, no "Why are you home, Jamie? Are you feeling okay, Jamie?" Just "Do something else for Princess Milan, please." I roughly grab the candle out of my mom's extended hand and stomp out of the room.

This. Is. Crap.

I tell you, I'm going to run away. There have to be other pumpkin patches in other towns, patches that want a hard-working, straight-A, uh, B, well, decent student, well-behaved, friendly, outgoing daughter. No one appreciates me here anymore. I should totally pack up my stuff and leave.

I throw open Milan's bedroom door and spike the candle onto her bed, volleyball style. I can smell her perfume lingering in the air and I want to get out of here as fast as I can. I head for the door but something catches my eye. Milan's little pink laptop is sitting on her desk, and there is an e-mail open in the window. I peek down the hallway. No one else is home but Mom and she's busy boxing up the candles. I quietly shut Milan's door and return to the laptop to read. It's a note from Uncle Jack, dated today.

Dear Milan,

It's great to hear from you. I'm doing well. We've been shooting some long days but I really think this movie will be a blockbuster. Darling, I know you're unhappy. I understand that you want to come home, I do. And of course I miss you. But we need more time. This is best for everybody. Talk to you soon.

Love,

Dad

Wow! Uncle Jack and Aunt Annabelle won't let Milan come back home. That's so weird. If she's that unhappy they should let her come home. Unless, of course, she did something *bad*. Oh my God, that must be it! Milan is involved in some scandal in Hollywood and her parents sent her here to hide from the paparazzi! It's brilliant actually. Who would ever look for Milan Woods on a pumpkin patch in Average, Illinois?

I rub my hands together, wondering what she did. Visions of late-night partying, DUIs, and shoplifting cross my mind. Well, there's one way to find out. I quietly slip out of Milan's room and head for my own. I'm going to change into my comfy clothes and get online. Milan's hiding here for some reason and I'm going to find out what it is.

15

Jamie?" Mom calls to me.

I jump at least two feet in the air. Shoot, I wish she'd stop yelling my name like that when I'm trying to be sneaky.

"What are you up to?" Mom asks.

I clear my throat. "Nothing. I'm going to lie down."

"What's wrong, are you sick?"

Oh, now she notices that I'm home sick. I fake a cough. "Yeah. A little."

"Okay, hon. But before you lie down can you help me carry these boxes out to the craft barn?" Mom asks.

Sheesh! I said I was sick and now she wants me carrying heavy boxes? What if I'm feeling lethargic and have a chill with a possible fever coming on? I shouldn't be hauling boxes. Where's the sympathy? Where's the chicken soup?

I walk down the hall and turn the corner into the dining

room. "I don't feel great, Mom," I say, sucking on the insides of my cheeks, hoping to look a little gaunt.

Mom looks me over. "Hmm. You do look pale."

I do? Bonus. I nod and throw in a sniffle for added effect.

"You should spend the day in bed. But first take a quick trip to the craft barn with me. Here, I'll carry the heavier box."

I sigh. "Fine." Whatever. At least I'll have the house to myself when I get back. Then I can research Milan and find out exactly what she did.

I pick up the smaller of the two boxes and follow Mom outside into the afternoon sunlight. She's going on and on about some new recipe she can't wait to try—something about a breadless bread. I don't even want to ask. It's bad enough that we've been eating so many freaky things, but now even the bread is on its way out the door too. What would happen if Milan didn't like pumpkins? Would we sell the Patch?

We walk in silence toward the craft barn and a few minutes later Mom swings open the screen door. The small copper bell hanging in the doorway chimes, letting everyone inside know that we are here. The overwhelmingly persistent potpourri smell of the craft barn slaps me smack-dab in the face and I scrunch up my nose. My eyes tear a little. I hoist my box up onto the counter next to Mom's and turn to face her. "Can I go now?" I ask, wiping my hands on my overalls.

"Yes, thank you, dear, that was a big help," Mom says, cracking open her box.

I nod and head for the door, antsy to get home.

"In a hurry?"

I fling around. Danny. "Oh, hey, Danny," I say. I feel kind of awkward since I breezed by him a short time ago when he was with Milan. He's standing near the back of the small barn, behind the huge rack of festive fall door wreaths, facing the wall and hammering a shelf above his head. His hat is on backward and the cutest tuft of hair is poking out over the plastic adjustable band.

"Going to work on your sprints some more?" he asks without looking up, still banging away on the nail.

My sprints? I furrow my brow. "What?"

"You know, for your track team," he says, pausing his hammering to look at me.

"Oh, my sprints." That's what Sara told him I was doing yesterday. "Yeah . . . no, actually I'm heading home. Not feeling so well." I unconsciously put my hand to my forehead.

"Sorry to hear that. Make sure you get lots of rest and fluids."

A tiny flutter starts in my tummy. Danny cares about my health. That's so sweet. Then again, maybe he just doesn't want me passing germs around. "I will," I say.

He picks up another nail from the box by his feet. "And by the way, your hair looks really nice that way."

Huh? What? What happened? Did Danny compliment me? I touch my hair, loose in waves around my shoulders. Well,

I do always wear it up for work. I guess he's not used to seeing me with my hair down. I feel myself begin to flush. "Um, thank you," I say, and then turn and leave the craft barn as fast as I can.

I practically float home on Danny's compliment. I know I shouldn't read much into it since he's got something going on with Milan, but it was still nice to hear.

Speaking of Milan, I let myself into the house and head straight for my room and my computer. I have at least a couple of hours before anyone else should be coming home, plenty of time to research Milan and the scandal that sent her to Average to ruin my life.

I launch a search engine and geez, Milan is all over the Internet! There is picture after picture of her doing, well, anything you can think of. Milan exiting a yoga studio. Milan walking a little yappy-looking dog on the beach. Milan walking on a sidewalk carrying a Starbucks. Whoa! Alert the media! She drinks coffee, people! Who even cares about this regular everyday stuff? I imagine having people taking your picture all the time must get annoying fast. I don't think I'd like it one bit. Of course, if people were randomly snapping my picture they'd probably find me sweaty and covered in pumpkin. Milan looks fantastic in every shot—even in the one of her outside a fast-food place holding a cellophane-wrapped hamburger. The caption says "Celebrities eat hamburgers too!" Really, they're wrong on two counts—(1) I don't think Milan is technically a "celebrity."

Her parents are; and (2) there is no way she was eating that hamburger. Getting ready to throw it at someone, distinct possibility. Eating, not a chance.

I've got to find something else on her though. Some explanation for why she's here. I'm pretty sure Uncle Jack didn't send her to live with us because we don't have a Starbucks within ten miles. The scandal can't be her caffeine habit. No, I have to keep looking and I'm sure I'll find whatever it is that she's done.

I click through several more search pages and *jackpot!* I click on the link titled "Milan Woods Sex Tape" and read. Hoo boy. No, she didn't! Well, yeah, according to this, I guess she did. Yikes, Milan.

Come out, come out, wherever you are, Milan Woods . . . Okay, people, have you noticed the perky blond offspring of Jack and Annabelle Woods has dropped off the face of the planet? Our SuperScoop.com reporters have the inside info on why our little baby bird has flown the nest. An insider close to Milan has informed us that Milan made a sex tape with none other than *Starling Light*'s Brandon Days! Her A-list parents were so horrified that they sent her to a hideaway to avoid the press. But she can't avoid us for long, can she, folks?

I skim through the rest of the Internet article, dated yesterday, and skip down to the comments. There are 144 and none of them are nice. People call Milan a spoiled rich brat, another child of celebrities gone bad, and some other not-so-nice names that question her virtues. Wow. I get the spoiled rich brat stuff, because, well, I know Milan and the description is fairly accurate, but I never would have guessed that she made a sex tape. That's gross! And then putting it online and showing people like she's so darn proud of herself. Yuck. I shudder.

Basically, Milan knew the story was about to leak and came here to hide from the paparazzi until it blew over. Who does she think she is, being so scandalous and then coming to my town and convincing people she's a good person, someone worthy of being our Pumpkin Princess? That is wrong. Well, I'm not going to sit back and let it happen. The contest is less than a week away. Someone has to teach Milan that life isn't all pumpkins and apple butter at the Patch. And that someone is me.

16

Up for any dinner, Jamie?" Mom says from my doorway. She leans in slightly, scanning the room.

I'm lying on my bed with my arms behind my head and my legs crossed out in front of me. I've been like this for the past hour, trying to decide how I should call Milan out and expose her for who she really is. So far I've got nothing. But I am starving since I'm not actually "sick" so I may as well get up. "Sure."

"Good, I made some soup," Mom replies.

I sit up, smiling. That was nice of her. And I love my mom's chicken soup. First she boils a chicken in a big stainless steel stockpot, getting all that fat off it and into the water. Then she takes the chicken out, throws in some onion, celery, and carrots, a couple of chicken bouillon cubes, and a box of acini di pepe noodles—those little tiny pasta balls. She sprinkles in salt and pepper and pulls off hunks of chicken and throws them back into the soup and then it's done. I've been watching her make it for years. It's the best.

I sit down at the table, my stomach growling. Milan sits directly across from me, and Dad takes a seat on my right. Mom sets a steaming bowl in front of me and my smile quickly fades. "What's this?" I point to the bowl of orange mush before me.

"It's a vegetable soup made with acorn squash and carrots," Mom replies, in a way-too-excited-about-soup tone.

"But it's not chicken," I say, stating what is already completely clear to everyone at the table.

"Vegetable soup is good for you, Jamie," Mom retorts. "Give it a try."

"But my cold," I continue. "It's chicken soup that's for colds..." I trail off.

Milan takes a big spoonful of soup. "Well, I think it's delicious, Aunt Julie."

"Thank you, Milan," Mom says, and looks at me. And then at my bowl of soup. And then back at me.

I guess she's waiting for me to try it. I put a tiny bit of soup on my spoon and bring it to my lips. It tastes mushy. And bland. And a bit lumpy. I try to look like it's not completely disgusting. Maybe if I added salt it would be better? I grab the salt from the table and shake it vigorously over my bowl.

"I already added a pinch of sea salt, Jamie," Mom comments.

Sea salt? Since when does Mom cook with sea salt?

"Yeah," Milan pipes in. "Too much salt isn't good for you, Jamie. It makes you retain water."

Of course. Milan must have turned Mom on to the sea salt. Well. If I'm going to retain any of this dinner I'm going to have to add something to it. "I'll be right back," I tell the table, and head for the kitchen.

I scrounge around in the refrigerator and find an almost empty bag of Oscar Mayer hot dogs on the bottom shelf. Hmm. The expiration date has rubbed off. I'm sure they're fine though. I nuke a hot dog on a paper plate, slice it, and then carry it back into the dining room with me. Once I'm seated I empty the paper plate into my bowl of soup. Milan gasps.

"What?" I say, looking up. Milan has one hand on her chest and Mom has her eyes closed, like she can't bear to see what I've done to her soup. Puh-lease. Milan makes a sex tape and we practically erect a statue of her in the middle of town. I put a sliced hot dog into my orange mushy soup and there's an uproar. Let's get a grip here, people.

I decide to ignore them, and take a bite of soup. Mom turns her head away from me. I look at Dad and I think I see a tiny smile start to come to his lips, but it's gone so fast I can't be sure.

You know, the soup isn't nearly as bad this way. I bet some ketchup would make it even better. But I don't dare get up for the ketchup. Not with Mom looking like I've just committed the world's worst sin.

Speaking of sins, I return my gaze to Milan. She's quietly

resumed eating her soup in between shooting me disgusted looks. I would love to tell her that if anyone should be shooting disgusted looks at this table it's me, and that I know about her gross tape so she can go ahead and step down from her high horse anytime now. And it's only a matter of time before everyone else knows too. We may be a small town but we have Internet access and we know how to Google. Surely someone will out her. It just can't be me. And not to my parents. I've been down that road before and they instantly jump to Milan's side. And if I make a big fuss calling Milan out in front of everyone in town they'll say I'm mean and jealous. Which I'm not.

"Did you have a good day today, Milan?" Mom asks, and then takes a slow sip of her water.

"Yeah, I did. I spent a lot of time at the concession stand this afternoon, making pumpkin spice lattes. We had a ton of teens hanging out and they mentioned they'd come by again after school lets out tomorrow. I think that's going to be a prime time for selling lattes," Milan says.

"Do you need help?" Dad asks her. "Jamie can come over to help you right after school."

I widen my eyes at Dad. No, Jamie cannot! Is he crazy, trying to stick me in a little concession stand with Milan all afternoon? "Um, I don't know how to make lattes," I say. There, that should get me out of it.

"They're a cinch, I could teach anyone how to make them," Milan says.

"Great, you can teach Jamie tomorrow," Dad concludes.

Well, all righty then. Thanks for asking me what I had planned for tomorrow afternoon.

"I'm going into town tomorrow," Mom says, looking at Milan. "Do you need me to pick up anything for you? Do you have what you need for the Pumpkin Princess contest?"

Milan thinks it over. "I think so. I already have a dress and my makeup and hair supplies. I don't think I need anything extra."

"Hey, I'm running for Pumpkin Princess too," I blurt out, and then feel slightly embarrassed when the whole table turns to look at me.

"Of course. We know that, Jamie. Do you need me to pick something up for you tomorrow?" Mom adds slowly, as if I'm hard at understanding or something.

"Um, no," I say. There's nothing I need and it's not like I can't drive myself into town anytime to get anything I do need.

"Samantha and April helped me fill out the Pumpkin Princess registration form so I think I'm good to go," Milan adds.

Huh? Who's April? Oh. She must mean Kettle Corn Girl. Geez, I've been calling her that for so long in my head I forgot she has a name.

"Luckily I had some head shots in my suitcase. I attached one to my registration form," Milan continues.

Head shots? I don't have any head shots. Though I did include a picture of me reading in the storybook barn and one from last year, of me and the Spinelli twins posing with their newly picked pumpkins. I hope that's good enough.

"Did you turn in your registration form, Jamie?" Milan asks, suddenly taking an interest in me.

"Yes, of course," I reply, annoyed that she's asking. I sent in my registration form as soon as I could. I wrote about how the Pumpkin Princess should be someone kind and good, someone who works hard every day at home, at school, and in the community. I said that the Pumpkin Princess should be mindful that the younger girls in town look up to her and want to be like her. That she should be responsible in her actions and behavior and not disappoint those kids. The Pumpkin Princess doesn't only lead the pumpkin parade and kick off the festival; she is someone the townspeople of Average should be proud to have represent them.

Milan grins at me. "May the best girl win, then."

I nod. "Yeah." Okay, so it wasn't the wittiest response but I couldn't think of what else to say.

Hmm. The contest is this Saturday. It's always two weeks before Halloween so that the Pumpkin Princess can also attend events around town like calling out bingo numbers at the senior citizens' center or cutting the ribbon at the Megastore. Which I've never understood. Seems to me the Megastore has a reopening once or twice a year but I don't recall it ever closing. Regardless, maybe I can nudge things along a little. I don't really have the luxury of time to wait for people to figure out Milan's scandal on their own. Truthfully, I'm shocked it isn't all over the Patch already.

"Speaking of the contest," Mom says, pointing her spoon at Dad. "Did you e-mail the schedule of events for the pumpkin festival to the town board Listserv? I'm sure they're going to want to get up flyers and put something in the paper."

"I e-mailed that weeks ago," Dad replies, furrowing his brow and shaking his head.

"All right, all right, don't get your socks in a twist. I only wanted to make sure."

"Been running this festival for twenty-one years..." Dad mumbles under his breath, and then shoves another spoonful of the soup into his mouth.

I put a hand over my mouth to cover my giggle and it hits me. E-mail. That's it! I can't publicly expose Milan to everyone in town but I can do it anonymously. I'll get into Dad's e-mail and retrieve the e-mail addresses for everyone on the town board. It'll be easy to break into Dad's e-mail. I've known his password practically forever: pumpkin. Then I'll set up an anonymous account, compose a message linking to the article about Milan's sex tape scandal, and hit Send. It's perfect.

17

I open my bedroom door as quietly as I can and listen. All I can hear is the clock on the wall in the front hall ticktocking away. The house is completely dark except for the flickering of the small angel night-light plugged into one of the lower outlets in the hallway. Milan went to bed over an hour ago and I heard Mom and Dad go to their room about twenty minutes after that. Everyone should be asleep.

I creep down the hallway, being careful to avoid the spot in the wooden floorboards in front of the bathroom that always creaks. A moment later, I reach Dad's small office. The walls are covered in pictures, mostly different shots from around the farm, but there is one of me when I was maybe two years old. My hair is in poofy pigtails and I'm sitting atop a huge pumpkin with both of my chubby hands wrapped around the pumpkin stem. Dad's desk is a total mess: papers and receipts and pens and paper clips and a big calculator are piled on top of one another in a chaotic-looking mountain, at least a foot high. I know not to touch any of it though. Even though it looks like chaos, Dad knows where each and every single thing is. And he knows when something has been touched. A couple of summers ago I came in here to snatch a few stamps from his plastic stamp dispenser and apparently I tossed the dispenser back on his desk five inches north of where he normally keeps it. The next morning he didn't yell at me or anything but he did make a point to tell me that the next time I needed something from his office, I'd better ask him first.

I take a mental snapshot of which way his desk chair is facing and then I slip into it, hit the Power button on his old computer, and wait. A few minutes later it's finally booted up. I keep checking the door, nervous that either he or Mom is going to wake up and catch me. I didn't turn any of the lights on though . . . so far so good.

I locate Dad's e-mail program and launch it. The sign-on pops up with his user name already typed in: HEdwards. I type "pumpkin" in the password box and I'm in. I scroll through his sent items, looking for his e-mail to the town board. Bingo. I launch the e-mail and it hits me, how am I going to get these addresses back to my computer? I scan Dad's desk and spot a pad of Post-it notes. I write down the e-mails as fast as I can, power off the computer, and check his office one more time to make sure everything is exactly like I found it. I creep back to my room with my list. Yes! This is going to work.

Once in my room, I take a seat at my own computer and launch a browser. I set up a Wow! Mail! account with the user name HelpfulFriend and type in the town board's e-mail addresses. I look over the names closely and I'm pretty sure at least five of these people are also on the Pumpkin Princess committee. This will be perfect if I can figure out what to say. It's tricky because I don't want to say too much, and risk someone figuring out it's me. But I do want them to know everything.

I sit back and stare at the screen. Hmm. In the subject box of the e-mail I finally type: "Our Pumpkin Princess?" In the message section I paste in a link to the SuperScoop.com article. That's good. Not too much but right to the point. I hit Send. There. Let's see them give her the green rhinestone stem now.

I rub my eyes and blink, adjusting to the sunlight streaming into my bedroom. I stretch my arms over my head and glance at the alarm clock. Two minutes before my alarm is set to go off. I love when I wake up right before it wakes me. I flick it off before it has time to buzz and I sit up in bed. I slept so good last night. I know it's going to be a great day.

I slip into my seat next to Dilly in math class. "Hey, Dill!" I say.

"Hey, girl," she says. "You're awfully chipper. Did Milan move back home or something?"

I laugh, shaking my head. "No, she's still living with us." For now, anyway.

"What's got you grinning like that? Is it a *boy*?" she teases. "Is it *Danny*?"

I feel my face flush.

"It *is* Danny then!" Dilly says, pointing at me. "What, did he ask you out finally or something?" Dilly reaches up and pushes a stray piece of bangs out of her face. She's got her bubblegum-pink hair in two Princess Leia buns today. It's pretty cute, I have to say.

"No," I insist. And it wasn't Danny I was thinking about. Not until just now. "I wasn't thinking about Danny," I add. "And he's not interested in me anyway. I think he has something going on with my cousin. Well, except for . . ."

"Except for what? Except for what?" Dilly asks, practically bouncing in her seat.

I shrug. "He did sort of compliment me yesterday. My hair, anyway." I reach up and run a hand through my hair. It's not interesting and unique like Dilly's, but it's pretty okay hair in its own right. "That doesn't mean anything though," I continue. "People compliment other people all the time and it means nothing." I pull out a notebook and begin doodling, emphasizing the nothingness of Danny's compliment.

"Not true," Dilly says. "Depends on how he said it. Did he

say, 'Nice hair, yo'?" Dilly juts both of her hands out in a criss-cross motion in front of her, like she might start rapping or something. She looks ridiculous.

I giggle. "Uh, no."

"Did he lean in really close to your face," she says, getting way too close to me herself, "his hot breath all over your cheek, and say in a low sultry voice, 'Your hair is like fine silk, Jamie'?"

A laugh erupts from me and I slap a hand over my mouth. "Dilly, you're so crazy," I say.

"Well, what did he say then?" she asks.

"I think he said my hair looked nice that day. Something like that."

"Huh." Dilly sits back and thinks about this. She looks back over to me. "Yeah, you're right. Could mean nothing."

I nod and turn to the front of the room as our math teacher walks in. That's what I thought. His compliment probably means nothing at all. But I wish it did mean something.

18

The last bell rings and I race home and change into my work clothes. I want to get out to the Patch as soon as possible and see what kind of mood Milan is in. I've been having the same glorious daydream all day today and I want to see if it came true. It goes like this: Milan is at the concession stand making lattes and showing off in front of Danny. He's there to get a water because he's so hot and tired from working hard, and not at all there to flirt with her. Not in my fantasy. Milan is batting her eyelashes and giggling at something Danny said when Mayor Hudson charges up to the stand, waving her Pumpkin Princess application over his head. "Never!" he shouts, his voice a thundering boom. "You will never be Pumpkin Princess of this town!" Milan gasps and dramatically clutches her chest with her hand. "I don't understand," she whimpers. But Mayor Hudson ignores her. He holds the paper in front of Milan and slowly rips it in half, letting both pieces fall to the ground. "Young lady, I strongly suggest you pack your things and leave Average. We are a town of moral people and you don't belong here." Milan gasps. "Y-you know?" The mayor nods slowly, his eyes narrow and full of anger. Even though the mayor doesn't say anything further he doesn't have to. Danny shoots Milan a disgusted look, sets the water down on the concession stand with a loud thud, and turns to leave. "Danny," she cries out. "Wait, I can explain!" But he keeps walking and never looks back.

Yeah. It's a good dream.

I reach the concession stand, half expecting Milan to be gone and Christy or Dana to be covering for her. But nope, she's standing there, full makeup, hair blown out, wearing a skimpy denim jumper. She's talking animatedly as she sets pumpkin spice lattes down before two girls.

Darn. Realistically I know it's only been maybe seventeen or eighteen hours since I sent the e-mail to the town board, but that should have been plenty of time for them to throw Milan out of the contest.

"So obviously I left that club," Milan is telling the girls. "Like I'm going to stay and dance at your club when you won't let in one of my closest friends, you know, Donna and Darnell Holtspring's daughter, Dara. Please."

The girls exchange glances, drop a few bills on the counter, and turn and walk away without saying a word to Milan.

I bite my bottom lip to keep from giggling. What's this? Are

Milan's braggy brag braggerson stories finally starting to bore people? Or do they know about Milan's sex scandal? Ooh, I hope they know!

"Hmph," Milan says, twisting up her lips as she watches the girls walk away. She looks at me. "What do you want?"

"Lattes," I say. "You're supposed to teach me how to make them this afternoon."

"Oh. Yeah. All right, well, don't stand there. Come back here and I'll show you how to use the espresso machine."

Ah, yes, I can sense this will be a fun afternoon.

Milan shows me three times how to fill the water chamber, grind the espresso beans, tamp them into the basket, and pull one or two shots. It's not quite as hard as I'd imagined. Steaming the milk, on the other hand, is a bit ridiculous. You have to hold this metal pitcher under the steaming wand and move it around and stuff just right to get the thing to steam the milk. Move it too far one way and it doesn't steam. Move it too far another way and you've got foam shooting out all over the place.

A group of girls approach the concession stand and Milan looks at me. "You make their drinks this time, okay?"

I nod and stand ready behind the machine.

"Hello, ladies," Milan calls out. "Lattes again?" Milan rests both hands on the counter, waiting.

I don't hear anyone speak so I lean back to get a good look at the girls. There are three of them, each one pretty, wearing matching soccer uniforms. They look older than me and I don't recognize them so I'm guessing they are from the community college. They're staring at Milan.

Milan lets out a nervous giggle. "Well? Something else then?"

The tall girl with the blond ponytail looks at her friends and then they suddenly burst out laughing and walk away.

Milan gives me an annoyed look. "What is wrong with people today?" she demands.

I shrug.

She sighs. "Make another practice one, I guess," she says. She walks over and hovers next to me, watching. I pick up the steaming pitcher, fill it halfway with milk, and start foaming. Milk shoots out of the pitcher and hits Milan square in the face.

"Argh! Jamie! How many times are you going to do that?"

"Sorry," I say. "I told you I wasn't good at this."

I spray Milan so many times trying to steam milk that afternoon that she finally asks me to not be her assistant any longer. Which is a fantastic idea to me. As far as I'm concerned I don't want to see her at all. Unless it's for her to tell me she's dropping out of the Pumpkin Princess contest.

I help Mom put the animals in the petting zoo to bed for the night and then stop at the corn maze to chat with Molly for a few minutes before I head home.

"How are the little ones doing today?" I ask.

She smiles. She loves talking about her brothers and sisters. "Good. They keep saying they want to come to the Patch to pick their pumpkins," Molly says.

"You should bring them," I urge.

Molly shakes her head. "Oh, I know you guys have the best pumpkins here but they're too expensive. We'll probably pick up some at the supermarket."

"Nonsense! You're not paying a thing. Bring the kids by," I say.

She looks surprised. "Really? That's so sweet of you, Jamie."

"Sure, it's no big deal," I insist.

"Kailey will be so excited. She's been cranky this week. Another ear infection," Molly explains.

"Is Kailey the three-year-old?" Danny asks, joining us at the corn-maze entrance.

I smile at him.

"Yeah, that's right," Molly says.

"My sister used to get a lot of ear infections at that age," Danny says. "Did you ever try lemon juice? I know it sounds weird but squeeze a bit of lemon juice in her ear and let it sit there for a few seconds and then let it leak out onto a napkin or something. I swear, it used to work on my sister all the time."

"Wow, no. We'll have to try that," Molly says.

"Ahhhhhh!" I scream, as I'm suddenly hit in the face with a large Styrofoam cup of ice-cold soda. "Wh-what . . ." I stutter.

"Whoops. Sorry," Milan says, not sounding sorry at all. "Guess I tripped or something."

I wipe the soda out of my eyes and glare at Milan. "You did that on purpose!" I yell.

"No I didn't. Get a grip, Jamie, you're embarrassing yourself. Besides, I think you look better covered in cola," she sneers. Molly and Danny are looking back and forth between the two of us, shocked.

The sticky liquid is seeping through my shirt and traveling down my chest *and* my back. It feels completely disgusting. "Excuse us," I say to Molly and Danny, and grab Milan by the elbow, dragging her away from them and behind the nearest barn.

"Ouch! Let go, you're hurting me," she whines.

Once we're safely out of earshot I turn her toward me and start yelling. "What's your freaking problem, Milan? Why are you so dang nasty to me all the time?"

"Oh please," she says, wiping at the spot on her arm where I had just been holding it. "Don't you have a big head."

"Me? You just threw a soda at me. On purpose!" I shout.

"That was an accident. Why don't you settle down?" she says.

"That was no accident. I'm not stupid! You don't even drink soda!"

This makes her pause for a moment. I got her. "Well, so what."

"So what? So what? So why have you been such an absolutely

horrible person to me since the moment you got here? I've tried and tried to be nice to you, but you're awful!"

Milan scowls, not backing down. "You want to know what my problem is?" she asks. "*You* are my problem." She points her index finger right into my sticky chest. "You and your pumpkin patch and your friends and your family dinners with your parents and your pigtails and your town. Grow up!" And then she stomps off toward the pumpkin field.

I stare at her back. What the heck was that?

19

Tuesday passed by quietly and so far there have been no problems today. Milan and I haven't said two words to each other since the soda incident and fight on Monday. I've been careful to avoid her as much as I can. And I've managed, luckily, to pretty much block out the new Milan merchandise all over the Patch. I know if I look at it too much my head will explode so I avoid it as much as I avoid Milan. It'll be gone soon anyway. If my plan works, that is.

After school, I head for the Patch. I'm supposed to be helping in the petting zoo today. I stop at Sara's booth first, my stomach growling.

"Jamie Special?" she asks with a grin.

I widen my eyes as she sets my favorite caramel apple in front of me. "Naturally," I reply, and take a giant bite. "Yum. Your store is going to rock when you open it. Of course, I'll go broke and gain twenty pounds from eating so many of the goodies you'll make."

Sara laughs.

I don't mean them to but my eyes wander to the dozen or so caramel apples sitting on display in the center of Sara's counter. The Milan.

I take another bite of my apple and chew. I swallow and nod at the apples. "You sure make a lot of those Milan apples, huh?"

Sara looks at the apples and rolls her eyes. "Dude, they are not selling! Never mind that they suck sticks. People don't seem to care that her name is on them. I would have thought those kids hanging all over her at the espresso machine would be lining up to eat 'Milan's favorite caramel apple.'"

"Yeah, really," I agree. I strain my eyes, trying to spot Milan at the concession stand. There are no people waiting for her to make a drink. She's leaning on her elbows with a blank stare, alone. I think this is the first time I've seen her doing anything alone here at the Patch. "Where are the kids though? The latte lovers? I don't see anyone hanging around Milan today."

Sara leans over the counter and strains to see Milan too. Milan looks up at us looking at her and sticks her tongue out. Sara pulls back off the counter and looks at me. "Wow, that was mature. Let's not make her any madder or she might give us cooties, and I'm all out of my anti-cootie spray today."

I grin. "It's weird though, right?" I say.

"Definitely," Sara agrees, sneaking a peek at Milan again anyway. "I wonder what's going on."

I stare at Sara for a moment, waiting. "Oh come on," I finally say. "You don't know?" I've been *dying* to tell Sara, but I wanted to see how long it took the news to reach her. Sara hears everything so I know when something reaches her it's a safe bet the town knows.

Sara gives me a quizzical look. "What?"

I can't hold out any longer. I reach into my front pocket, pull out the folded article, and smooth it on the counter for Sara to see. I ripped it out of the *Exposure* magazine I bought at the gas station this morning.

Sara lets out a low whistle and nods. The article is titled "Another One of Hollywood's Kids Goes Bad" and there's a blurry photo of a naked Milan and Brandon Days on what looks to be a plaid blanket, and there are black boxes covering up their private bits.

Sara glances back at Milan. "That's nasty."

"Totally," I say. "Oh well, it's not my problem. I better get to work." I wave my caramel apple at Sara and head for the petting zoo.

There are toddlers swarming the goats when I get there. Kids love to feed the goats and these guys will eat all dang day if you let them. I watch the parents stick their quarters into the bubblegum-looking machine and the children catch handfuls of goat feed as it falls out of the silver tunnel. They hold their offerings out to the goats and squeal as their palms get licked clean. I grab a bucket and walk around the pen, picking up dropped brushes. We keep a bucket of brushes at the front, by the gate, so the kids can brush the goats. They never remember to put the brushes back, however, and instead drop them all over the place. I walk to the back of the pen and kneel down to swipe some brushes into my bucket. I hear some girls talking about Milan on the other side of the fence, and I look up in alarm. But I don't move. I sit quietly, straining to hear what they're saying.

"She's so gross!" the first girl says.

"Total skank," the second girl agrees.

I tilt my head toward them to try to hear better.

"They need to fire her before they lose business," the first one says.

"Oh, definitely," the second one replies. "I'm so not going to buy anything that *she's* touched."

I lean even closer to the fence, trying to hear more but the girls have moved away. Shoot. I hadn't thought about Milan's scandal hurting business.

A little stunned, I walk back out to the front of the goat pen, set the bucket of brushes down, and let myself out. I walk about twenty feet away until I can get a good view of Milan at the concession stand. She's leaning on one hand and looking incredibly bored. There are still no people anywhere near the stand. Is this because of the sex tape scandal? I almost thought the opposite would happen and that at least the guys would be lining up to buy something from Milan.

This is weird. Even if people don't want lattes someone always wants a soda or a bottle of water. The concession stand is never entirely empty. This isn't good.

I work in the petting zoo for the next hour but I know I'm not doing as good a job as I can. I'm totally worrying about what's going on. Why is everyone avoiding Milan like this? It's not as though you can catch making a sex tape like a cold or something. What if that one girl was right and Milan's making the Patch lose business instead of gain business? That would be ridiculous, right?

Ugh. I feel kinda icky. I don't *really* want to hurt Milan, do I? She's still my cousin, no matter how big of a butt head she is. I almost feel like a bully. And I'm not a bully!

But it's not my fault so I should try not to feel bad. It was only a matter of time before people found out anyway. Even if I hadn't e-mailed . . .

I can't take it anymore. I need to find out what's going on. I tell the other zoo workers that I'll be back shortly and start walking through the Patch. I'm not sure what I'm looking for exactly. I'm trying to figure out if people are avoiding Milan because of the sex tape thing. I stop in front of the haunted house. Hmm. It's always fairly dark in here. I'll go sit in a corner and eavesdrop for a while.

I slip in the front door and feel my way through the dark house until I reach the kitchen. This is as good a place as any to hide. The kitchen of the haunted house is decked out in gory goodness—the sink is full of blood, there's a pot on the stove with a fake head sticking out of it, and there is a pair of legs arranged in the oven so that you can see the soles of the feet pressed up against the glass. There are fake blood spatters all over the walls and glasses of water with eyeballs floating in them left on the kitchen table like someone had been drinking there. I tuck myself behind the refrigerator and wait for people to pass by.

A few minutes later I hear Kettle Corn Girl walking through with Hannah, the girl who sells tickets to the haunted house out front. They must be on break.

"Do you think Milan will still run for Pumpkin Princess?" Hannah says.

"I wouldn't know," Kettle Corn Girl replies.

What? What does she mean she wouldn't know? She helped Milan fill out the registration form herself.

"I thought you two were friends," Hannah says in an accusing tone.

"Whatever gave you that idea?" Kettle Corn Girl returns. "I barely know the girl."

Oh my God! What a liar! She's been all over Milan since the minute Milan started working here. Unreal.

I wait a few minutes after the girls have left and then slip out into the daylight. I can't believe this reaction is solely from the tape. Of course I was hoping they'd kick her out of the Pumpkin Princess contest. And maybe I wouldn't have minded if people hung on her every word a little bit less. And I sure wouldn't shed a tear if all that Milan merchandise went away. But I certainly didn't want the whole town to shun her.

I try to shake off the guilt and remind myself that Milan did this to herself. I mean, she *made* a sex tape. Like all the other silly rich Hollywood kids have. Hello, attention much? I'm sure Milan's just waiting for Mark Burnett to give her cell a ring and offer her her own reality show. Gag. This is totally, 100 percent not my fault. It was completely inevitable that the town would find out.

That feeling in the pit of my stomach is telling me otherwise though.

❧

I step into the house and scan the living room and hallway. I'm not sure what I expect to see—maybe Milan freaking out and throwing things against the wall or something. But it's quiet.

"Jamie?" Mom calls. "That you? Can you set the table? Dinner's almost ready."

"Uh, yeah, Mom."

I walk into the kitchen and gather the plates and utensils. I briefly glance at the disks of baked dough covered in brown mush sitting on the baking sheet on the stove. I'm not even going to ask.

"Butternut squash personal pizzas with fresh rosemary," Mom tells me anyway. "Don't they look delicious?"

"Mmm," I say, hoping that will satisfy her question so I don't have to tell her what I actually think. I walk into the dining room and set the table. A few minutes later we're all sitting around the table and no one is saying a word. Just chewing. I sneak glances at Milan when I think no one is looking, but she continues to stare at her plate and pick at her food.

Mom finally breaks the silence. "Everyone have a good day?" She slices off a piece of pizza and puts it in her mouth and waits.

Dad nods.

"It was fine," I say.

We all look at Milan. Nothing.

"Do you like the pizza?" Mom asks her.

Milan nods but doesn't look up.

"What about you, Jamie?" Mom asks.

Me? Well, it tastes like bland baby food slathered on extra-thick cardboard. But I can't exactly say that. "It's fine," I say instead.

For the next few minutes the only sound is the four of us sawing off pieces of our mushy pizza.

"Are you girls getting excited for the Pumpkin Princess contest?" Mom asks us.

I shoot a look at Milan and hold my breath.

Milan raises her head. "I'm dropping out of the contest," she says, her voice flat.

I gasp and then slap a hand across my mouth. I didn't mean to react like that.

Milan's eyes linger on me for a moment and then return to my mom's.

Mom stops eating. "But why? I thought you were looking forward to it."

Milan shrugs. "I don't think it would be appropriate considering the current circumstances."

Dad wipes his mouth with a napkin and pushes away from the table. "Sounds like female talk," he says. "I'll be going." He picks up his John Deere hat off the hallway table, slips it on his head, and walks out the front door. I look at his barely touched pizza. He's probably going out for a burger.

Milan watches Dad leave too and then turns back to us. Her expression is different. Almost embarrassed.

Oh man, I wonder if Dad knows too? I guess it's possible that one of the people on the town board told him. Especially since everyone else seems to know about it.

"Milan, what's this about?" Mom says, her voice full of concern now.

Milan leans back in her chair and folds her arms over her chest. "To put it simply, gossip. A stupid rumor has been spread through town that I participated in a sex tape with Brandon Days."

"Oh my lord," Mom says, horrified.

"It's not true, Aunt Julie," Milan adds quickly. "I've never even met Brandon Days let alone made any kind of movie with him. It's total fiction."

"How did this happen?" Mom asks.

"Oh, you know how those stupid online gossip sites are. They just make stuff up half the time. I think they were trying to create a juicy story for my sudden disappearance from Hollywood. Like it's any of their business." She sighs. "So someone made a fake movie and threw it online. I looked it up when I first heard the rumor. It's totally not me. The girl in the movie has a huge butt." Milan looks at my mom's reaction to this. "Not that that's important at this moment. But seriously, if you look at the date stamped on the movie it was made while I was here in Average with you guys. It's not me."

What? No way! I never even thought to look at the movie. I mean, ewww, why would I? But if it's not even Milan . . .

"Why didn't you say something?" I ask Milan. "You should defend yourself. Tell people. Write a letter to the Web sites that posted the story."

Milan laughs. Loudly. "Sorry, Jamie," she finally says. "It was what you said about writing to the Web sites. That would never work. It would only make things worse."

"That's libel, Milan, what they did to you," Mom says.

"Yeah. I don't think anyone actually cares," she says. "From my experience it doesn't even matter if what the online sites or tabloids say about you is true. Once it's out there people believe it hook, line, and sinker."

"That's terrible," I mutter. I feel horrible. Really horrible. I can't believe I caused this whole mess and Milan didn't even do it!

Milan shrugs. "It's nothing new. I'm used to it." She carefully slices off a tiny piece of her pizza and resumes eating.

Mom shakes her head. "What an awful thing to get used to. There has to be something we can do—"

"Wait," I interrupt. "Don't drop out of the Pumpkin Princess contest. I'll fix this. I promise."

Milan looks at me like I'm an idiot, but I'm not kidding. I *will* fix this. Maybe it's not entirely my fault. Celebrity gossip does spread awfully fast. But I feel partially responsible and while I can't make a difference on a widespread level I can make a difference in Average. I know I can. I excuse myself from the table and go to my room to get to work.

20

I wake up Thursday morning raring to go. Today's mission: spread the truth about Milan around Average faster than the flu. First step is to e-mail the town board again as Helpful Friend. This time I apologize for the regrettable mistake and add that the sex tape is a fraud and that Milan was here in Average with us when it was filmed.

At school I tell anyone who will listen to me about my poor cousin Milan getting framed. I make sure to keep repeating how impossible it would have been for her to have made the tape in the first place. This is our solid undeniable proof and it has to get around fast. I even tell Joyce, the lunchroom monitor, the story. Joyce is pretty gossipy so I figure it will only help in getting the news spread around town.

After school I head straight for the Patch, but before I go to work, I have to make a stop. I get in line behind a mom with two kids. When it's my turn I step up to the register and order. "Hi, one raspberry sno-cone and a bag of kettle corn, please."

Sno-Cone Sammy and Kettle Corn Girl eye each other as they put together my order. What? So I never usually stop at this booth. Can't a girl change up her after-school snack once in a while?

Sno-Cone Sammy hands me my sno-cone.

"Thanks," I say. "Oh wait, maybe I should bring Milan a sno-cone too, you know, to cheer her up. You got any flavors back there with no calories, no preservatives, no additives . . . Uh, well, maybe you should just fill up one of those paper cones with some plain ice shavings."

Sno-Cone Sammy looks concerned. "How's Milan?" she says in a low voice.

Perfect. I was hoping she'd ask me that. "She's okay," I say slowly. "As well as you'd expect, considering the lies spreading all over town about her."

"Lies?" Sno-Cone Sammy inquires, obviously hoping I'll spill, which of course is my plan.

"Yeah. You know," I say, and lean in close, "about the t-a-p-e." I'm not sure why I felt I needed to spell that out.

"It's not true?" Sno-Cone Sammy asks, and then flips around to look at Kettle Corn Girl. "See? I told you Milan would never do that."

"Oh God," I say, "of course it's not true. Milan doesn't even know Brandon Days. And if you look at the date stamp on the movie you'll see it was made while Milan was living here in Average."

"Really?" Kettle Corn Girl says, moving closer to us.

"Yes! And I have no reason to defend Milan, she doesn't even like me," I add.

"That's true," Kettle Corn Girl replies.

Ouch.

"Well, I never believed it for a minute," Sno-Cone Sammy says, shaking her head for emphasis. "April kept saying it was true, but I couldn't see Milan doing something like that. It's not her."

"She wouldn't," I agree. "Thanks for the food, guys." I drop some bills on the counter. I take my sno-cone, the ice, and the kettle corn and head for home. I need to change and get back out here to work.

Mom asks me to be the break reliever this afternoon, which, really, couldn't be any more perfect a job to fit in with my plan. It gives me a chance to tell everyone I relieve about Milan being framed with the sex tape. I tell Jeff and Teegan at the pumpkin chucker, Petey and Hannah at the haunted house, and Kate and Laurel at the funnel cake stand. I know my plan is going to work and people will forget this stupid story about Milan and go back to, well, I guess worshipping her like they were before the rumor leaked. But even if they are worshipping her it's better than them ignoring her and making fun of her behind her back for something she didn't do.

My last stop is to see Sara. She's straightening up the display case when I reach her.

"Hey, where've you been? No apple today?" Sara asks.

"Nah, I had kettle corn and a sno-cone," I say.

"What? Since when? I think I'm insulted." Sara fake-pouts and I laugh.

"Don't worry, it was a one-time thing," I insist.

"It better be. I don't like throwing away my creations." Sara picks up the Jamie Special and acts like she's going to throw it in the trash.

"Whoa, whoa, whoa," I say. "Let's not be hasty. I'll take it home."

She grins. "I knew you would." She hands me the apple and leans over the counter to glance at the concession stand. I look too and see Milan busily making her pumpkin spice lattes. "Did you hear?" Sara asks me a minute later.

"Hear what?" I turn and face her.

"About Milan's sex tape being a fake?" Sara says. "Someone set her up. That wasn't her in the movie. It was someone else."

"That's terrible," I say, faking shock and disgust. "Even Milan doesn't deserve that!" Yes! If Sara has already heard the news I've been telling people then it must be spreading well throughout the Patch.

Sara nods. "Even though Milan has been so dang rotten it

still must be hard being a kid with famous parents. Those gossip sites and tabloids don't attack only the celebrities, they attack their whole families."

"Yeah," I agree. Sara's right. I never thought about how hard it must be for Milan to have such famous parents.

21

Good morning!" a cheerful voice sings from behind me.

I back out of the refrigerator, a strawberry yogurt and an apple in my hands, and shut the door with my hip. "You talking to me?" I say.

"Of course!" Milan smiles. "It's a nice morning, isn't it?" she asks. She pulls the refrigerator door back open and roots around inside for her soy milk. I'm still standing in the middle of the kitchen, shocked that Milan is being, well, pleasant.

"Um, yeah. Seems like a good morning." I slip the food into my backpack and zip it closed. "You're in a better mood," I add.

Milan spins around. "You know, I really am. I like it here. You have a nice town."

Wow! What a change. A lot different from what she said when she first got here. I smile. "Yeah, it is. It's a great town."

"Back home," she continues, "people never would have

believed the truth about me and that whole stupid rumor. But here? Everyone believes me. It's refreshing."

I smile. She thinks everyone believes her because she said so. And I'm sure some do. But I think mostly it's because I told absolutely everyone I could and it spread. But I'm not going to say anything. It's not like I need to brag about what I did.

"That's great," I say. "Well, see you later, I'm off to school." I head for the door.

"Jamie, wait," Milan says.

I turn back around and raise my eyebrows.

"Can you help me after school in the concession stand? My latte crowd has returned. I could use the assistance."

I scrunch up my face. "You know how bad I am at making lattes though . . ."

"I'll teach you again," she urges. "It'll be fine. You'll get it."

I think about it. Maybe this is a step in the right direction for Milan and me. "Well, all right. See you after school," I say. As I head out to my car I feel myself smiling. That was the nicest exchange I've had with Milan since she arrived.

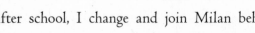

After school, I change and join Milan behind the espresso maker. I've only sprayed her with foam twice so far and I think I'm getting better. And don't get me wrong, it's not like we're friends or anything now. I'm not delusional. Milan is just less mean to me.

I'm rinsing out the espresso shot glasses when Danny steps

up to our stand. His brown curls are mussed and I can see a short piece of hay sticking in his hair, right by his left ear. He looks amazing.

"Hey, ladies." He nods at both of us and I feel my insides get mushy. "Can I get a soda?"

"Sure," I say. I pull a can of Mountain Dew out of the cooler and hand it to him, hoping he doesn't think it's weird that I know his favorite soda.

"Are you doing anything with that Baby Boo?" he asks me, nodding toward the back of the booth.

"Oh my God," Milan whispers loudly in my ear. "Is he really going to flirt with you in front of me like that?"

I feel my cheeks flush and I look over at Danny's face. He's grinning.

"Milan!" I hiss, wanting her to shut up now.

"What?" she says. "It's totally rude!"

I pick up the tiny white pumpkin off the table at the back of the booth and carry it over to Danny. "Here, you can have it," I say.

"Thanks," he replies. "My kid sister loves these."

"Sure," I say. After he's left I turn to Milan. "For future reference, a Baby Boo is a type of pumpkin, *not* a pet name. Well, I'm sure it's someone, somewhere's pet name but it isn't mine. And Danny wasn't flirting with me. He doesn't even like me."

"Oh. Bummer about the name. It was sorta cute," Milan says thoughtfully. "But I wouldn't say that he doesn't like you."

"Oh, I'm positive," I say. But now I'm wondering what Milan's deal is. Why would she think he likes me? Not that it wouldn't be freaking fabulous if he did like me, but we both know that he doesn't. He likes her. What about those lunches and the short-shorts and the tractor rides?

Well, he *did* give me a tractor ride once too. Back when I was fifteen and first learning how to drive a car. Dad let me ride around out in the field with an old truck and I got it stuck in a big mud patch. Danny saw me and gave me a ride back to the house to get Dad. But that was it. He was only being nice then. It's not like we have moonlit rides around the Patch or anything. It's not the same as how it is with him and Milan. He doesn't look at me like he looks at her. No one looks at me like that. Boys want to kiss Milan. They want to stack pumpkins with me.

I can't say any of this to her though. I don't think Milan and I are at that place yet. "Can you show me how to grind the espresso beans again?" I ask, changing the subject to something that doesn't make me blush the shade of a tomato.

That evening Mom, Milan, and I are lingering at the dinner table, chatting over Pumpkin Surprise, which, go figure, I've come to sorta like. Mom must be slipping me something in my 2 percent milk (I may like the Pumpkin Surprise, but they'll never get me to touch that soy stuff). I can tell she is absolutely tickled that Milan and I are actually kinda getting along.

"I can't believe the Pumpkin Princess contest is tomorrow," Milan says excitedly.

"You're going to do it?" Mom and I ask at the same time. Geez, with all the drama I almost forgot about the contest.

Milan nods. "I never officially dropped out, so what the heck."

"Awesome! May the best girl win, then," I say, echoing what Milan said to me when she first found out I was in the contest too. But I mean it. I want to compete against Milan, fair and square.

22

Oh, Jamie." Sara puts a hand on her cheek and looks me up and down. "You are absolutely beautiful."

"I am?" I ask tentatively. "Beautiful" isn't a word I hear too often to describe me. I walk over to the full-length mirror on the back of my bedroom door and stand in front of it. A tiny gasp escapes my lips. "Oh my God. You're a miracle worker, Sara!"

"No, I'm not," Sara insists. "You had all the material. I just combed and twisted some hair and brushed some makeup on in a few places."

I stare at my reflection. Sara has part of my blond waves pulled back from my face and gathered into some twisty thing on top of my head and the rest hanging in loose curls. I'm wearing my dress: an emerald sleeveless fitted number that ends in a ruffle a few inches above my knees. She's accented my eyes to match the dress and blushed my cheeks a shimmery shade of peach. And I'm wearing lipstick. I've never put anything but Chap Stick on my lips before. And that was only in the winter.

"I can't believe it's me," I say, shaking my head.

"Well, it's definitely you. And you're going to go out there and win Pumpkin Princess. You deserve it, Jamie."

I blink rapidly, tears beginning to fill my eyes.

"Oh no you don't," Sara says. "Do *not* cry." She waves her hands in front of my eyes. "I practiced those eyes on myself for over two hours, trying to perfect the look. I saw it in *Seventeen*. It's absolutely flawless right now and I don't want to chance having to start over."

I take several deep breaths. "Okay, okay. I won't cry. It's only, I've wanted this for so long. I can't believe it's here. It's like a dream."

Sara puts a hand on my shoulder and squeezes. "I know you have. And you'll do it today and you'll win. And then you'll dream a new dream for yourself and go after that. It's not like anything is truly ending today."

I nod, even though I can't help feeling sentimental thinking about all those days I wandered the pumpkin patch as a kid, a broken pumpkin stem tied on my head, pretending to be the Pumpkin Princess.

"Are we ready to go?" Sara asks, packing the makeup in a bag to take with us.

"Almost," I say. "Would you mind waiting for me out front? I need to do one other thing before we go."

"Sure." Sara lets herself out of my room and I head for my closet.

I kneel on the floor and root around in the back, careful not to mess up my hair on the clothes hanging overhead. There. Got it. I straighten up and head for Milan's room.

I knock softly on Milan's door and hear her tell me to come in. "Jamie! You look fabulous," Milan says.

"Stunning," Sno-Cone Sammy agrees. I notice Kettle Corn Girl is nowhere in sight. Good. Milan obviously figured out her number.

"You look amazing yourself," I tell Milan. And she does. Almost like a pink Barbie princess doll. Her hair is in big fancy curls and her pearly pink lips are in a huge, completely perfect smile.

Milan tilts her head slightly and says, "Thank you." And I think she genuinely means it.

"I stopped by because I have something for you," I say. I pull my present from behind my back and hold it up in front of me.

"My Roy Vances!" Milan shrieks, grabbing her cheeks in surprise and then racing over and pulling the shoes from my hands. "They're perfect! How did you get them cleaned? They were ruined!"

"I didn't throw them out when you told me to," I explain. "Instead I saved them and worked on them with some saddle soap my dad has. And voilà, good as new."

Still clutching her shoes, Milan throws her arms around me and gives me a big hug. "Thank you, Jamie."

I hug her back. "You're welcome." Milan and I never did talk about that awful fight we had behind the barn that one day. And I don't think we ever will. It just happened and we moved past it. For the first time since Milan arrived she actually kind of feels like a sister.

I pull away. "Well, we both better get over to the contest. I'll see you there, okay?"

Milan nods, still admiring her shoes. "Good luck!"

"You too," I reply, and leave her room, heading for my own.

In my room, Mom is sitting on the bed. "Oh, Jamie, honey, you look gorgeous."

I feel myself blush. I don't know how many more compliments I can take today. This is so out of my comfort zone. "Thanks, Mom. It's all Sara. She fancied me up."

"I think it's all you. You've always been beautiful," Mom says.

"Aw geez, Mom," I say, embarrassed.

"Come sit by me for a minute, hon."

I walk over to my bed and take a seat next to her.

"How's Milan doing getting ready?" she asks.

"Great. She looks stunning. Which is no surprise of course."

Mom nods and gives me a small smile. "Good."

I feel like she wants to say more, but is holding back.

"Mom?" I begin, and she nods. "Why is Milan living with

us anyway? And don't tell me she's on a break again. That makes no sense. She's been here all this time and doesn't hardly ever talk to her parents or anything."

Mom lets out a heavy sigh and furrows her brow. I can tell she's not comfortable with telling me the truth. She sits quietly for a few moments and then speaks. "Milan's had a tough time back home. Her world is turned upside down there. She needed some time away."

"Why though? What could be so bad?" I press on.

I can tell that Mom is struggling with how much to say. She's never liked talking about other people—especially family. But she finally relents. "Well, I guess I can tell you. Your father and I thought it was better you didn't know. We didn't want you thinking poorly of your family. But don't say anything to Milan. She'd only be embarrassed."

I nod.

Mom shakes her head. "That brother of mine. He's been having an affair with some young Hollywood actress from his last movie. The girl is only *two years* older than Milan. It's despicable."

My jaw drops. I saw that movie and I know who Mom's talking about. She's a kid!

"Annabelle found out about it and instead of Jack dumping the girl and sticking with his family, he left Annabelle. She was trying to hold on to him and at the same time started abusing pain pills. I guess she wanted to be numb." Mom must have taken in the shock across my face because she starts to speak faster. "To sum it up, Annabelle went into rehab and Jack knew he couldn't take care of Milan so he asked if she could stay with us." Mom glances at my closed door and then leans in toward me. "But between you and me, I think he just didn't want to. He wants to be free to have fun with his new young girlfriend. It's such a shame."

"It's horrible!" I exclaim. "I can't believe Uncle Jack did that to Aunt Annabelle."

"And to Milan," Mom adds. "Poor girl is a mess. She gets no attention from her parents at home and she so desperately craves it. Your dad and I have tried as hard as we could to shower her with attention. But we know it doesn't replace getting it from her parents."

I think over the past weeks. All the crazy meals we've been eating. All the sucking up Mom and Dad have been doing to Milan—telling her what a great, hard worker she is. And Dad comforting Milan that day by the giant pumpkin. It makes sense now.

And I feel terrible. Poor Milan. "It explains a lot," I tell Mom. "It explains all that showing off she was doing around the Patch."

Mom smirks. So she's noticed it too.

"And running for Pumpkin Princess," I add.

"You know, Jamie, you're a lucky girl. You have a family and loads of friends who adore you. And you have a good heart.

I know how much you want Pumpkin Princess today, but even if you don't win it, you're always a winner, sweetie."

"Can I get some nachos with that cheese?" I tease.

Mom laughs. "Okay, okay, so I'm cheesy. But parents are allowed. I think it's part of the aging process. You'll be cheesy one day too, dear."

"I doubt it," I reply.

"I love you, Jamie," Mom says.

"I love you too," I say.

Mom stands up and smooths out the mocha-colored silk shirt she's wearing. "Ready to get over to the contest?"

"Um, not yet. I have one more thing to do. You go ahead, and tell Sara to go ahead too. I'll be there in a few minutes."

"Okay, sweetie, see you there," Mom says, and leaves my room.

Just as I'm about to shut my bedroom door I hear Dad cough from the hallway. He's wearing a denim collared shirt and his only pair of dress slacks and he's staring down at the carpet with both of his hands shoved in his pockets.

"Dad?" I say.

He finally looks up, and lets out a low whistle. "Wow. Jamie, you look..." He pauses and smashes up his lips. I turn my gaze away, feeling awkward. "You look beautiful, honey."

I look back at Dad, blinking. "Really?" Dad has never ever, ever told me I looked beautiful. Never.

He nods. "You're growing up."

"Well, yeah," I say. We stare at each other for a few uncomfortable moments.

"And that stuff your mom said about you," he says, "goes for me too. You're a good kid." With this he reaches out and pats me lightly on the shoulder.

Wow. This is probably the nicest exchange Dad and I have ever had. Before I can think about it too much I throw my arms around his waist and squeeze, and he hugs me back.

A few seconds later Dad stiffens up and pulls away. "Well, I'll let you finish getting ready then. See you out there." He smiles at me and walks down the hallway, toward the front of the house.

I shut my bedroom door, grinning to myself. I walk over to my full-length mirror and look at myself one last time. It's amazing what Sara has done for me. I reach up and pull out the thingy holding my hair up in the fancy twist and watch my hair fall onto my shoulders.

23

I pick up a couple of hair bands and quickly tie my hair up into two pigtails. I slip out of my dress and carefully lay it across my bed. It's so pretty and I don't want it to wrinkle. I pull on my overalls and head out of my room, toward the front door. As I'm wrapping my hand around the doorknob I look up and see my reflection in the oval mirror on the wall. I forgot to wash off my makeup, but I like it so I'll leave it.

I jog to the far north side of the Patch where the giant stage is, and the mass of folding chairs filled with people from town waiting, eager to watch the contest. There is a big white banner stretched above with PUMPKIN PRINCESS painted in large bubble letters across it. Strands of green and orange twinkle lights wrap around the poles at each corner. The heavy burlap curtain is pulled shut across the stage and I imagine the contestants are in the closed tent off to the side, doing last-minute fixes to their hair and makeup. I wonder if anyone has even noticed that I'm not there. Sara is probably worried and searching everywhere for me. But she'll figure out soon enough that I've dropped out of the contest. And I know Mom will understand. They're both right, Mom and Sara. I don't need this contest. Nothing is ending for me today. I'm going to keep dreaming bigger dreams for myself. Maybe I would have won Pumpkin Princess and maybe I wouldn't have. All I know is that it doesn't really matter because I don't need to win it. Not like Milan does. And I'm here to support her.

I slip in and out among the people standing at the very back of the audience, chomping on their kettle corn and sipping their hot apple ciders. I find an empty seat in the last row, close to the exit, and sit down. I'm pretty far from the stage, but I'll still be able to see. About three rows up from me sit two young girls, maybe eight or nine years old, both wearing those plastic princess tiaras that you can get at the dollar store. They're giggling and straining their necks, trying to get a good look even though nothing is happening at the moment. They remind me of me at that age. I scan the backs of heads near the front until I spot Mom and Dad's. They're leaned in close like they're discussing something. I spot Sara standing off to the side, scanning the crowd. She looks at my mom and shakes her head and shrugs. She must have told my parents that I didn't show up. I shrink down into my metal folding chair, not wanting them to see me until the contest is over.

Mayor Hudson points at his wife from the bottom of the stairs and Laurel nods and hits the Play button on the giant boom box sitting on the edge of the stage. She holds a microphone up to the speaker and the music starts. Mayor Hudson takes center stage, a second microphone in hand. He loves emceeing the contest. Each girl—there are five in total—walks across the stage in her formal dress as he introduces her. Milan is the second one out and she looks fantastic. There is a huge smile across her face and the crowd has obviously moved past her sex tape scandal. I clap and cheer along with everyone else.

A few minutes later the mayor is talking to the first girl, Jayna Williams, while the other girls wait backstage. He asks her what Pumpkin Princess means to her and she snatches the microphone from his hand and launches into a monologue. About three minutes in, people start to shift uncomfortably and the mayor keeps throwing looks out into the audience, unsure of how to tie up Jayna's answer. He slowly starts to wrap his hand around Jayna's to pull the microphone away from her face.

"...and like the pumpkin," she says, speaking quickly now, not willing to let go of the mike, "full of hundreds of unique pumpkin seeds, no two of which are alike, our town of Average is full of unique and talented individuals, and I would like to be your pumpkin."

Mayor Hudson snatches the microphone from her and the

audience is quiet. She wants to be our pumpkin? A few people in the crowd let out giggles.

Jayna leans back into the microphone in the mayor's hands. "Er, princess. Your Pumpkin Princess. Thank you."

The crowd claps politely and Jayna disappears behind the curtain. Milan comes out for her turn to answer the same question and I whistle and clap for her.

"At first, I didn't really want to be Pumpkin Princess," Milan begins, carefully choosing her words. "At first, I didn't even want to be here at all, to tell you the truth. I thought things were better back in L.A., where I'm from. Average is so, so different from back home. But I've come to find out that different can be good. Really good. Your town is so warm and inviting and accepting. You've made me feel like a real part of it and it would be an honor if I was able to represent your town as Pumpkin Princess."

I put a hand on my chest and blink back tears. That was the most sincere I've ever heard Milan. The crowd claps and I eagerly join in.

"I'd bang that," an old scruffy guy sitting in front of me says to his friend.

Huh?

"Um, what?" I ask loudly. I lean forward in my seat, sticking my head between the two men. "What did you just say?"

The men look at each other and then laugh.

Me? I'm seeing red. "I thought I heard you say you'd 'bang' Milan Woods, and that is wrong on so many levels." I rise to my feet. "For one, she's seventeen years old, you old perverts. Two, she's a real person with real feelings, not just some picture in a tabloid. And three"—I'm practically shouting now—"she's my cousin, you creeps! If there's going to be any banging around here it's going to be my hand up against the side of your face!" My heart is racing a mile a minute and my hands are clenched into fists. I feel like I could slug these two morons. And I haul pumpkins every day. It'd hurt.

"Settle down, doll," the friend returns, and the guys continue laughing at me.

"Doll? Oh, you're really asking for it." I push up my sleeves like I'm going to do something and then I feel a hand on my shoulder.

"Need some help, Jamie?" Danny says.

I look up at Danny. His eyes are fixed on the two men. He's angry. I've never gone for that whole fairy-tale prince rushing up to save the helpless princess thing but I have to admit, at this very moment, Danny is even hotter than usual.

"These jerks are saying disgusting things about my cousin," I tell him.

"Well now, that's not very nice," Danny replies. "Sounds like they need to cool off a bit." He pops off the plastic lid of the Big Gulp Mountain Dew he's holding and pours the contents, ice and all, over the two men's heads. I cover my mouth and giggle. I know exactly what that feels like.

"Ah!" the men scream, dancing around and shaking off the soda. They yell out some curse words at Danny.

"This is a family place, gentlemen, and we don't allow that kind of talk. You can be on your way or I can escort you out," Danny says.

Everyone around us is staring at these two losers, waiting to see what's going to happen. The men grumble some more, but they get up and quickly leave.

I turn to Danny, a smile creeping over my face. "That was awesome."

Danny shrugs.

"I can't believe those jerks were talking about Milan like that," I go on. Of course that's why Danny got so mad. He was probably defending Milan's honor.

"You're a good friend to your cousin," Danny says. He's looking at me so hard I feel like my legs might give out.

I hold his gaze. His hazel eyes look an amazing shade of green right now. "Well, those guys were obnoxious. I wanted to shut them up."

"I don't mean now, with those idiots," Danny goes on. "I mean with the contest. You were running for Pumpkin Princess too, and you probably would have won it. But you dropped out to let Milan win, right?"

He thinks I would have won? That's so sweet! "Um . . . um," I stammer. "Well, yeah, I wanted to support Milan. But I doubt I would have won anyway."

"I would have voted for you," he says.

I feel myself flush down to my toes.

"Milan is one of those girls who needs a lot of attention," he continues. "And you're not. You're a great girl without needing the world to constantly tell you that you are."

I'm in such total shock over the nice things Danny is saying to me that someone is going to have to come by and sweep me up off the floor with all the little stepped-on pieces of kettle corn.

"Wow. Thank you," I reply softly.

Danny gives me a huge smile, our eyes still locked. "Hey," he says, "after all this Pumpkin Princess hoo-ha is done, do you want to maybe, I dunno, go get one of those pumpkin latte things with me?"

What? Is he asking me out? It sounds like he is. Oh my God!

What do I do? I've practiced this moment a thousand times in my head on the off chance that it might ever actually happen. And now here we are and he's asked me out and he's waiting for my answer. And *oh my god*, I'm making him wait for my answer! Say something! I don't trust myself to speak so I nod.

24

The contest continues. Each girl does a solo walk around the stage to show off her dress, recites a fall poem, and shares her best pumpkin recipe. Milan's is my mom's Pumpkin Surprise. After the last girl has gone, the audience votes on the slips of paper that were already on our chairs when we entered and passes them to the aisle for the committee to collect. I vote for Milan of course.

There's a fifteen-minute intermission while the votes are counted. I watch Danny walk toward the big brown barn where the tractors are kept. He's probably going to help Burt Schafer hook up his fancy-looking tractor to the big red hay wagon that pulls the Pumpkin Princess after she's crowned. My dad used to pull the Pumpkin Princess wagon, but a few years ago Mr. Schafer had a mild midlife crisis, I guess you'd call it, and did his own version of *Pimp My Tractor*. His John Deere has wheel spinners and undercarriage neon lighting. And I'll admit, the shooting orange flames on the red paint job are kinda cool. But I don't get the big red metal roll cage at all. I mean, he farms corn.

"Jamie! Jamie! There you are," Milan says, moving toward me as fast as she can in her ultra-high heels.

"Huh?" I can feel the big stupid smile still lingering on my face as I turn to look at Milan, but I don't care. I still can't believe Danny asked me out.

"Where've you been? You missed the contest! The ballots have been turned in and the Pumpkin Princess committee is tabulating the votes right now. And where's your dress? And why is your hair back in those pigtails?" She scrunches up her nose and waves her index finger at my hair.

I take a deep breath, thinking about how to reply to the list of questions she rifled off. "Here. I know. That's okay. At home. And because this"—I point to my head—"is me."

Milan blinks rapidly, totally confused. "Okay, hold up. Tell me why you missed the contest."

I sigh. I have no idea what to say to this question, at least not·to Milan.

Milan's eyes dart over my shoulder to the stage. The girls are walking back out to join the mayor, already waiting. "Forget it," Milan says. "Let's go."

Milan tugs my arm hard and the next thing I know I'm being dragged toward the stage.

"Milan!" I yell. "Milan, stop! I don't want to go up there." But she isn't listening to me. She keeps tugging me forward. And she is a lot stronger than I thought too. Maybe she's started loading the pumpkin chucker herself recently and I haven't noticed.

I look at the people sitting on either side of the aisle as Milan pulls me to the front. There's the Spinelli family. The twins see me and point. I wave with my free hand. And oh wow, Dilly did come. She was supposed to babysit her little brothers today. She's sitting with Sara. Sara is staring at my hair in horror. All her work destroyed. I reach up and touch one of my pigtails. "I'm sorry," I mouth to her. We're almost to the stairs and I see the middle school librarian in one of the chairs on my left. Everyone in town really is here. And yikes, my parents have spotted us. But I wouldn't say they look mad. Surprised maybe.

Milan starts to ascend the stairs and I plant my feet firmly. Well, as firmly as I can. "No," I say. "I'm not going up there. Look at me, Milan."

Milan looks at my overalls and pale pink T-shirt and shrugs. "You're the one who put that on. Let's go." She gives one last big tug and I half fall, half walk up the stairs onto the stage.

The contestants are giving me puzzled looks and I bite my bottom lip. I can't explain why I'm up onstage ruining their big moment right now. The most I can do is try to sneak off. Milan's grasp on me has loosened and I make a break for the back of the stage.

"Not so fast," she says, looping an arm through mine and pulling me into the line of girls with her. "Sorry, Mayor," she says. "You can continue."

The mayor is standing in the center of the stage with the microphone poised under his chin. He's giving us a strange look. "Um, okay," he says, and turns to face the crowd. "Let's get on with announcing Pumpkin Princess, then."

I turn sideways and try to hide myself partially behind Milan. I don't know what Milan is doing, but I feel completely ridiculous up here in front of the town like this.

"We have carefully tabulated the votes, and this year's Pumpkin Princess is—" the mayor begins.

"Hold it," Milan shouts out, and walks up to the mayor. "I'm sorry, Mayor, I guess I was lying before when I said you should continue. I have to say something." She pulls the microphone from his unresisting hand. I think he's in shock. The people in the audience are probably thinking it's typical Hollywood bad behavior to do something so rude as interrupt the crowning of Pumpkin Princess.

I look at it as my cue to get the heck off the stage. I start for the back of the stage again when Milan's voice booms over the speaker system.

"Jamie Edwards, you stop right there."

Aw geez. Did she have to do that? I turn around and face the audience again. I try to smile.

"I'd like to officially drop out of the Pumpkin Princess

contest," Milan announces, and there are several gasps in the audience. "I know, I know," she continues. "Only minutes ago I told you how much of an honor it would be for me to represent your town. And I wasn't lying about that, it would be a *huge* honor. I've come to love Average. But"—she takes a deep breath—"there's someone who loves Average even more. I don't deserve to represent your town. If you want someone who is hardworking, and true, and confident in herself, someone who *is* Average, Illinois, then you want my cousin Jamie Edwards." Milan swings her arms out in my direction.

Oh my God. I'm so touched! And embarrassed. And minorly horrified. But mostly touched. I can't believe she just did that. I feel tears spring to my eyes and I can hear the audience cheering. I walk to Milan and give her a big hug. "Thanks, Milan. That's the nicest thing you've ever said about me," I whisper in her ear.

"I mean it," she whispers back.

The mayor steps up to Milan and plucks the microphone out of her hand. "Done now?" he asks. He looks irritated. I don't think he liked Milan's interruption too much.

Milan nods and puts a confident arm around my shoulder.

"Like I was saying before, this year's Pumpkin Princess winner is . . ."

I hold my breath.

"Molly Jenkins."

My eyebrows shoot up. Oh! Molly! She's perfect.

"What? The girl with the unibrow?" Milan says a bit too loudly.

"Milan!" I scold.

Milan gives me a sheepish look. "I mean, yay."

I can't help it, I start to giggle. And Milan joins me. I can't believe for even a second either of us thought I could be crowned Pumpkin Princess after not even participating in the contest and charging up here at the end in my work clothes. It's ridiculous.

The mayor looks at us and I bite the insides of my cheeks to keep from laughing. Milan and I watch as he places the green rhinestone stem on top of Molly's head and the crowd claps. I scan the audience until I see Molly's mom, and her brothers and sisters bouncing up and down in their seats clapping for their big sis, and I wave at them.

When it's over, Milan and I head for the steps. On the way down from the stage Milan says, "Hey, Jamie, you want to go throw corn at people?"

I smile. "Not just now. I'm off to get one of those fancy lattes."

25

Best latte ever. It'll become "our drink." We'll serve lattes at our wedding. Years from now I'll be sitting at the kitchen table with our grandchildren, telling the story of how we went for lattes on our very first date. I'll show them the plastic coffee stirrer that I've saved all these years and they'll aw at their romantic ol' gran.

Of course, I'm getting ahead of myself. But it was a darn good coffee. I ordered the large so Danny and I could spend as much time as possible together and I tried my hardest not to do or say anything lame. Well, except for one small thing. I did mention that YouTube video of the cat that can sing "La Bamba" and after I said it I thought, "Wow, I could have come up with something much better to talk about." But he said it sounded interesting and he'd definitely check it out. So maybe it wasn't the lamest thing ever. And he *is* picking me up to go to the cineplex in half an hour for our second official date.

I pick up my dark eyeliner pencil and line my right eye again, trying to make it look more like the left. Hmm. Looks pretty straight, I think. Corner to corner at least. This wearing makeup thing isn't so bad once you get used to it.

Milan walks into my bedroom and flops onto my bed. "Excited about your date?" she asks. I smile at her. Things have been going good with us. I wouldn't say they're perfect. She still has her snippy moments and I'm sure I still have my annoying moments for her. But we're both trying and so far it's been really nice.

"Borderline delirious," I reply, and she laughs. Pumpkin season technically ended this week, but Milan is still living with us. Mom talked to Uncle Jack and Aunt Annabelle and they said that Milan could stay with us for the rest of the school year. Yep, Milan Woods is now attending Average High School. And loving it! And not that I'd ever tell Milan this but I'm loving it too. I'm going to get to see what it's like to have a sister after all.

"You two do make a sweet couple," she says.

I blush. I think we make a sweet couple too.

"You're not going to do your eyes like that, are you?" she asks suddenly, and I shake my head. Though I totally planned on leaving my eyes exactly like I have them. She sighs. "Here, let me help." She heads for the pile of makeup on my desk and pauses in front of my window to peer out.

"Paparazzi?" I ask sympathetically. They sure have been driving Milan nuts the last couple of weeks since they discovered she was living here with us.

She nods. "They're thinning out though. Only a couple of them are hanging around still. And they'll get bored soon enough. Soon as the next Hollywood celebrity gains ten pounds or the next sex scandal hits."

I think about her dad's affair with that young actress and wonder if she's thinking about it too. It hasn't hit the papers yet, but it's likely only a matter of time. I wonder if she's furious with her dad or worried about her mom. If she misses one or both of them or if she misses home and her friends. But she doesn't seem to want to talk about it yet. Any of it. She hasn't even mentioned her parents once actually. Not since she found out that she could stay with us. I'm sure she's dealing with everything as best as she can and when she's ready to talk I'll be here.

Milan wipes my face with a makeup-removal pad and redoes my makeup from top to bottom. I think she's being a bit dramatic—my makeup wasn't that bad. I thought I had a good handle on the blush, personally. But if it makes her happy I'll let her show me again how to do it.

She puts the finishing touches on my lips, a quick swipe with a glittery gloss—for lips that beg to be kissed, she tells me, and I can feel my cheeks flush again. I'd *love* to kiss Danny but I'm not sure we're there yet.

I hear Danny's truck rolling up outside and I stand and tug at the bottom of my sweater. "Do I look all right?" I ask Milan.

I see her eyes narrow like she's about to say something like "Yeah, for a country girl," but she presses her lips into a smile instead. "Yeah, you look great. Have a wonderful night."

I walk out to the living room to meet Danny, and see my mom standing at the door talking to him. I don't see Dad anywhere though. He must be holed up in his office. He probably can't even bear to think of me dating, let alone get the visual.

"You have her back at a decent time now, okay, Danny?" Mom says, trying to look serious.

"Promise," Danny says, and nods.

He holds the screen door open for me to pass by him and we head for his truck. My right hand fidgets with the purse strap on my shoulder. I've never carried a purse before and it feels weird. But Milan said I had to bring one so I have someplace to put my lip gloss in case I need to reapply. Which I hope I don't. It's hard keeping it in the lines on my lips. She also said I had to stop carrying my cell phone in my back pocket and that I should put it in my purse too. She said no one looks good with a lumpy butt. And I guess I'd have to agree with that.

We walk silently down the gravel driveway to his truck, our feet kicking up rocks with each step. I'm about to ask him what movie he wants to see tonight when I feel his hand slip into mine. And I think my heart may explode. His hand is large and warm and a little rough with calluses from the work he does, but I don't care. It could feel like grade-fifty sandpaper and I wouldn't mind one bit. It's perfect. I glance up at him and he looks down at me and smiles. And I go for it. I'm not sure where it comes from but I tug him toward me, step up on my tiptoes, and kiss him. And he kisses me back. All these years of waiting and I've finally decided I don't have to wait anymore.

Acknowledgments

If I could, I would give a green rhinestone stem to the following people:

Janine O'Malley, my fabulous editor

Kerry Sparks and Elizabeth Fisher, my awesome agents

Deena Lipomi and Mandy Morgan, my fantastic critique partners

And to my wonderful family and friends for their continuous love and support

Thanks, guys!